THE GIRLS THEY LOST

THE AUCTION TRILOGY

J. H LEIGH

To the one who always feels like sunshine on my soul
no matter how dark the storms of my life rage...

CONTENTS

COPYRIGHT

THEY GIRLS THEY LOST

By J.H Leigh

NEWSLETTER SIGN UP

Want to stay updated on future releases from J.H. Leigh? Of course you do! Here you go, just click the link and follow the instructions. Thank you! CLICK ME TO SIGN UP!

A NOTE FROM JH

Dear Reader,

The saga continues. There was so much personal growth for the girls in the midst of horrifying situations that I was beside myself with love for these poor girls.

Confession time, I cried while writing this book. There are parts of this story that are so stark, so poignant that I couldn't help but sob.

I hope you're ready for the next wild ride because it doesn't stop or let up for one second.

The third book, THE GIRLS THEY FEAR, is coming soon.

All my love,

J.H. Leigh

BACK COVER BLURB

Dead girls don't run or tell secrets.

Nicole, Dylan and Jilly may have escaped the horrors of the auction house but they aren't safe.

Madame Moirai has eyes everywhere. There's nowhere the girls can go that can shelter them for long. On the run, with no one to trust, it's just a matter of time before they're found.

Enlisting the help of a disgraced NYPD detective turned private investigator with demons of his own and a sociopathic criminal kingpin, the girls will discover just how far they're willing to go to take down Madame Moirai.

All they have is each other — and a dogged will to survive.

But will it be enough?

1

I knew I was dreaming but it didn't stop the dread as I approached the body lying on the stainless steel slab. A white sheet draped over what I knew to be Tana's form.

I knew it was her because I'd already lived this nightmare.

I was the one who found her down in that cold basement of horrors, the one who set fire to Madame Moirai's auction house so me, Jilly and Dylan could escape in the dead of night with nothing but the flimsy clothes on our backs.

As much as I wanted to walk out of this room, the dreamscape wouldn't let me go.

Sheer exhaustion will do that to you.

Don't do it.

Dream me, much like the real me, ignored the advice. My cold fingers plucked at the sheet, pulling it away from Tana's face.

Death had muted everything vibrant about Tana. Her wild mane of red hair lay flat and dull against the slab as if it would be disrespectful to shine when she was hollowed out. The subtle wrinkle in her lips gave away the dehydration while the deathly pallor of her skin was appropriately macabre for the situation.

A handful of days ago, Tana had been alive, naively innocent and hopeful for a better future.

Hope...what dangerous fucking lure for kids like us.

They'd known exactly how to push our buttons, how to shut down that little voice of reason cautioning us to run away so we'd fall neatly into their trap.

If low-level anger was constantly percolating in my soul before taking Madame Moirai's deal, now full-baked rage was my constant companion.

I stared at Tana, tears welling in my eyes. This was some bullshit.

A stranger would never know by looking at her

corpse how nice she'd been. How desperately willing she'd been to save her grandmother, even if it meant selling the only thing she had of value: herself.

Fuck them all for being the soulless bastards they were.

What kind of monster took a beautiful butterfly-like Tana and squashed it beneath their feet without thinking twice about what it was taking from the world?

My level of grief might've suggested we were besties, that we'd known each other for years but six days ago, I hadn't known Tana at all.

But trauma binds people in ways that time never could.

Within minutes of meeting the bubbly girl, I could tell she was the kind of person who always tried to find the best in people even if she had nothing to base her opinion on. She just *wanted* people to be the best version of themselves and how could you not like a person like that?

Again, hope raised its ugly head. Nobody ever talked about the price of caring too much.

Or being helplessly naive and trusting.

I wasn't one of those people. Neither were Dylan or Jilly. But I'd fallen into the same trap as Tana, which told you just how brilliantly manipulative Madame Moirai's network was.

We'd all taken the deal but Tana had somehow ended up dead. Who killed her? Her buyer? Madame Moirai? Who?

I should've known better than to think the deal was anything more than an elaborate con but the money had muzzled my gut instinct.

The thing was, good con artists knew how to manipulate their marks.

And fuck, were we manipulated.

I stared a moment longer at the Tana in my dream, silent tears welling in my eyes.

I wish I could've saved you.

I started to reach for an errant curl and Tana's eyes popped open. Bloodshot green eyes stared with accusation and all I could do was stare back in horror. Her mouth dropped open in a silent scream that I heard in my head with the violence of shattering glass. I jumped back with a start, awakening in the car with arms flailing.

Dylan yelped as she cast an annoyed look my way. "Jesus, you okay?"

I wiped at the sweat on my upper lip. Just a dream but everything about our reality was just as fucked up. Tana was dead and we were on the run from Madame Moirai and some shadowy network called The Avalon.

We didn't know what the fuck we were going to do or how we were going to survive but we weren't going to just lie down and die for their convenience.

If need be, we'd go down scratching and clawing, and at the very least making them wish they'd never approached us for the deal.

The odds weren't in our favor. We were likely going to die no matter what we did because no one was going to protect us from the ultra-rich assholes who wanted us dead.

To Dylan, I muttered, "Not even a little bit." She didn't press. She knew; None of us were okay. Not after everything we'd been through. We would never be okay. I glanced in the backseat. Jilly was curled up, sweatshirt bunched beneath her head, fast asleep.

I slumped further in the seat and exhaled a long breath. I used to think nothing could be worse than the life I had before signing my contract with Madame Moirai but I was wrong. By comparison, my life with my booze-soaked mother, Carla, seemed a fucking cake-walk right about now.

"So where are you taking us?" I asked. Dylan supposedly had a place where we could hole up until we figured out our next move but details were pretty sketchy and I wasn't sure if I trusted the bitch. "How do you know it's safe?"

"Isn't anything safer than out in the open?" Dylan countered.

"Cut the crap, Dylan. Just tell me where we're going," I said, irritated.

"It's an underground network for runaways run by a guy I used to know. We should be safe there."

"An underground network? What do you mean?"

"Fuck, enough with the questions, detective," Dylan snapped. "If you've got a better idea for hiding out, I'm all ears. If not, just shut the fuck up and enjoy the ride."

Dylan wasn't going to win any personality awards but I didn't have a solution that trumped hers so I had no choice but to zip my trap and let her take the wheel. We were forced together by circumstance, not because we liked each other but there was safety in numbers.

Supposedly.

"We're going to have to ditch the car when we

get to the city," I said, sighing. "For all we know the car's already been reported stolen."

"I know someone who can take care of that," Dylan said. "We can even get a little cash for it, too."

"Illegal chop shop?" I surmised. Dylan nodded. I shrugged. "Fine."

I would miss the car. I'd grown up in the city, was used to public transportation but having a car to ourselves felt like safety, even if it was only an illusion.

At this point, beggars couldn't be choosers, you know?

I needed to cling to whatever boosted my mental stability because I felt as if I were teetering on the edge of a total break down.

Becoming some kind of hero had never been in my career trajectory.

"So what were you dreaming about?" Dylan asked.

"Tana."

"That sucks."

I glanced out the window. "Yeah. I can't seem to shake the last image of her from my head."

"I'm glad I didn't find her," Dylan said but in a rare show of empathy, added, "I'm sorry, that's gotta be really shitty."

It was but it was my fault. I had to find Tana before bailing. I could've saved myself and took off into the night but something held me back. I wouldn't have been able to forgive myself if I'd left the girls behind. I never realized how burdened I was with an overabundance of conscience but I sure found out in a trial-by-fire sort of way.

"So you've got no one who will start asking questions when you show up missing?" I asked.

"No, but isn't that the point? I can't imagine Madame Moirai would single out girls people actually care about. Seems messy."

I agreed. "Except my best friend Lora would care. She might start asking questions. I should call her."

"Don't do that," Dylan said, her tone sharp. "It'll just put your friend in danger."

"You think they're watching the people in our lives?"

"Hell yeah. Especially now that we're dangerous loose ends. If you've got people they can get to, the best thing you can do is lay low for now." She cast a quick look my way. "Who did you put down on your form as your contacts?"

"No one. I didn't want them contacting my mother for anything. I left that line blank."

Dylan nodded. "Me too."

But there was an odd cadence to Dylan's tone. Everything about Dylan always felt a little left to center but I didn't have the mental energy to keep digging. Dylan could keep her secrets. We all had skeletons.

"How do you think Madame Moirai finds her marks?" I asked, curious. "My buyer knew things about me that weren't public. Confidential information, you know?"

"Yeah. I know. They must have access to records, maybe through social services or the cops. You ever been arrested?"

"No, but social services had a file on me when I was younger. My mom was pretty shitty in the care department. When I was six years old, she took off for a few days and there was no food in the apartment. The next thing I know, people are showing up to collect me and I went into a foster home for a few weeks. After that, my mom was more careful to at least try to make an effort, not that she was any good at it." I glanced at Dylan. "How about you?"

"Cops. I've been arrested a few times. Petty theft, mostly shoplifting. I have a record of misdemeanors, nothing felony, though. I worked hard at keeping my theft small so that all charges would drop off when I turned eighteen."

Shoplifting was nothing. If it weren't for Lora's parents feeding me plenty of times, I would've had to steal to eat. Food shouldn't be a privilege. A kid should never face the threat of starving to death. So yeah, shoplifting, *whatever*.

But that did raise a troubling question: did Madame Moirai have crooked cops working for her?

All signs pointed to yes.

"We're so fucked," I murmured.

To which Dylan didn't disagree. "Makes you wonder what happens to a human being that they are willing to do what they do to kids without losing a night's sleep."

"I don't know but I fucking hate them."

"Same."

"I want to make them pay. Somehow, someway."

"We have to survive first."

Dylan was right. Dreams of vengeance would have to wait until we were in a safe place. We needed allies, people willing to help us, people unable to be bought.

But did those people even exist anymore?

It seemed everybody had a private price tag on their integrity these days.

Even us.

Except without knowing it, we'd sold ourselves out for clearance aisle prices and those fuckers had laughed at our stupidity.

I closed my eyes, swallowing the bile.

Their time would come.

Somehow.

I'd make sure of it.

2

Dylan surprised us when she announced, "We need to hole up for a day or two. I need to do some recon."

"What do you mean?" I asked, confused. "What happened to your contact who could help us?"

"It's fucking complicated, okay? I need to check it out first and see if the conditions are good. The environment changes a lot in The Runaway Club. I'm not about to walk into a fucking trap."

"What is this, the Hunger Games for runaways?" I asked with a dark glower, not for the first time questioning Dylan's ability to come through. When Dylan glowered in response, I huffed a short, aggrieved breath and shrugged. "Whatever. And just where exactly are we supposed to hole up while you do this recon?"

"We have cash, we can pay for a motel room," Jilly piped in. "It would be nice to have a shower and a bed."

"We shouldn't spend the money. We have no idea when we'll be able to get more," I said.

Jilly released a pouty sigh. "Fine. I think I might know of a place we can stay for the night. It's not great but no one will think to look for us there."

"Where?" I asked, curious.

"It's an old church. Supposed to be torn down at some point but I don't know, I guess the money dried up or something because now it's just empty and every thinks its haunted or something."

"Is it?" I asked.

"Not that I can tell but I don't really believe in that stuff anyway."

"Me neither," I said, but the idea of staying in a creepy abandoned church didn't fill me with excited butteries. "Where is it?"

Jilly leaned forward between us, answering, "It's on Wheeler and Tenth. You can't miss it. Big gothic structure. I mean, if you're into that thing, it's really kinda beautiful. Fun to draw."

"You draw?" I asked, surprised.

She shrugged. "From time to time. Hard to get my hands on materials but when I can, I like to play around. I'm not very good but who cares, right? I'm not looking to open a gallery."

Dylan followed Jilly's directions and we pulled around the back of the church, off the main street so the car wasn't immediately visible. Trash clogged the gutters and the area wore depression like a cloak. The church itself was creepy as fuck. "Easy to see why people think this place is haunted," I murmured, gazing up at the blackened and aged spires. If I had a choice I wouldn't want to walk inside either.

"Isn't it beautiful?" Jilly asked with a dreamy expression.

"This looks like where the devil holds mass," I retorted, glancing at Dylan for her opinion but Dylan had other things on her mind, obviously bigger than the scary old church.

Shouldering her pack with a clipped, "Let's go" Dylan trudged toward the warped back door, using her shoulder to force it open.

Jilly, almost giddy, followed and I, having little choice, filed in behind, hoping that ghosts weren't real and we weren't about to be murdered by a cantankerous ghoul with issues against the living.

The cold, dank air in the church smelled of decay and rot — and possibly dead things — and I almost double-backed to take my chances in the backseat of the car during the night. "We'll freeze in this decrepit old church," I said, shivering. "It's not like we can build a fire or something."

"There's a room off the pulpit for the deacon. It's got carpet and some old blankets. We'll be fine," Jilly chirped.

Dylan and I shared a look before I said, "Jilly... have you been here before? Like as in, stayed here?"

Jilly shrugged. "A time or two. I like it. And no one bothers you here. It's a safe place."

Of all the shitty-ass apartments Carla had plopped us down in, with drug addicts loitering in the stairwells, screams echoing in the hallways, and pedophiles leering from every angle, each one of those places seemed like Mr. Roger's neighborhood in comparison to this rotting hulk of broken faith. And Jilly felt at *home* here?

That said a lot about her childhood.

Not for the first time I was pretty sure sweet Jilly was a closet sociopath. *Holy fuck, remind me to stay on her good side.*

Dylan smirked, gesturing, "Lead the way" and Jilly skipped ahead, humming to herself as she went. As we entered the main hall, bats and other winged things rustled in the darkened alcoves, reminding us that we weren't alone. We passed by disintegrating pews slowly being eaten by time and neglect, our steps echoing as they crunched on debris that ranged from broken glass to shards of wood.

Jilly opened the door to the right of the pulpit and made a grand gesture as if she were showing us to a luxury hotel suite with all the amenities. "Ta-da! Look at that. A nice squishy sofa, blankets, and the carpet isn't too nasty."

"It's the goddamn Ritz," Dylan remarked, glancing around as she let her pack slip from her shoulders. "I ain't sleeping on that floor. That's for damn sure."

"We can all fit on the sofa if we get cozy. We'll need the body warmth anyway," Jilly said, shutting the door and placing a chair beneath the doorknob. At my questioning look, she said, "No sense in taking chances. I'm not the only person who knows about this place."

"If you hadn't done it, I was going to," Dylan said, approving. To me, she said, "Break out the food. I'm starved."

I dropped my own pack, rummaging around for some food. We'd raided the house in upstate New York for provisions so at least we had something to put in our growling bellies. I tossed bags of chips to each of the girls and then ripped into my own. I felt bad for robbing those poor people but what choice did we have? None. It was Madame Moirai's fault for turning us into thieves.

It was late afternoon, the light filtering through the grime-crusted windows cast a yellowish glow on everything. Even in forgotten squalor, the stained glass windows in the highest alcove managed to whisper of a better time, when it was a new, shining jewel in the congregation's crown.

"I wonder why the church is abandoned?" I asked.

"Oh! I know that answer," Jilly said with self-importance, her eyes twinkling with excitement. She didn't wait for our encouragement, starting in with a mini-history lesson whether we liked it or not. "Well, it was built in 1853 for like, thirty grand, which was a lot of fucking money back then."

"Right now, I'd love to have about thirty large in my pocket," I quipped, tossing a few chips in my mouth. "That's at least half of what that bitch Moirai owes me."

"Like we're ever going to see that money," Dylan returned and I agreed but Jilly was annoyed.

"Hello? In the middle of a story?"

I gave her some semblance of an apologetic smile,

which she accepted, continuing with the same excitement.

"Anyway, so yeah, when it was built, it was like the grandest thing people had ever seen. It's built with blue stone, sandstone trimming as well as Caen stone for the altar and font. It was legit pretty fancy."

"All for sinners and hypocrites to gather around and feel good about themselves," Dylan said, unimpressed. "Religion is a fucking scam."

I agreed with Dylan but I didn't want to rain on Jilly's parade. "So why'd it close?" I asked.

"Over the years, it just fell out out favor. People left the congregation when bigger, better churches were built. Eventually, the repairs cost more than the archdiocese wanted to spend and it was closed down with the vague hope of refurbishing but it never happened. Last I heard, it was scheduled for demo but that obviously hasn't happened yet." Jilly shrugged. "Maybe some religious history nut is trying to save it, who knows."

"Why do you have such a hard-on for churches?" Dylan asked. "Are you super religious or something?"

"You don't have to be religious to appreciate pretty things. Churches are always beautiful. I could give two shits about the people in them. I just like the way they look."

Legit answer. At one time, this place was probably just as awe-inspiring as Jilly thought it was. For me, churches weren't sanctuaries and I was guessing by Dylan's scorn, she didn't think much of churches either but we were both judging the place by the people in them.

In my experience, die-hard religious people were just as rotten as the pews out in the great hall. I was willing to bet every single one of Madame Moirai's buyers put on a good show of praying to a God they didn't believe in just so they could buy a teenager to fuck and break later behind closed doors.

I released a pent-up breath, rolling my shoulders. To Jilly, I said, "How many times have you spent nights here in this old place?"

"Enough."

"Was this your runaway spot?" I asked.

Jilly shrugged. "One of them."

Speaking of runaway, I looked to Dylan. "What about you? When you going to meet up with your contact?"

"As soon as it gets dark," Dylan answered. "Easier to slip in and out when it's not blazing daylight."

Made sense. I curled up on the sofa, tucking my legs beneath me. I didn't want to think of the bugs or critters probably making their home in the dusty couch because I didn't want to sit on the floor either.

Silence was the enemy for all of us. Too much quiet made us think of the shitstorm we were facing. I'd never felt so alone in my life. Even having Dylan and Jilly here with me was a small consolation when I wanted to bury my head in my hands and sob.

"How long do you think Madame Moirai has been buying girls?" Jilly asked in a small voice.

The fact that it was almost automatic that we all were thinking the same thing was a testament to the trauma we'd endured. Each of us still had bruises on our bodies from our time with our buyers that were slowly fading but the mental damage would last a lifetime.

"I don't know," I answered, resting my chin my knees. "Something tells me they've been doing it for a while. That morgue was set up like a professional business. They wouldn't have that kind of attention to detail for a one-time thing."

"What were they going to do? Kill us in our sleep?" Dylan asked.

Jilly supposed, "Maybe poison? Something

slipped into our food? That seems easiest and less messy than like, shooting us, right?"

"Heroin overdose," Dylan answered flatly. "If anyone found our bodies, they'd just assume we were junkies because kids like us...we're all obviously drug addicts, too."

"I've never done drugs," Jilly said, offended. "Not even pot."

"It doesn't matter. No one asks questions when a girl in the system shows up dead. Easy to write off as a tragic statistic of a fucked-up childhood." Dylan swore beneath her breath, anger painting hot spots on her cheeks. "Fucking bastards."

I nodded. "I'm scared to think of how many girls are dead because of them. It makes me sick to my stomach that they're going to get away with it. They know no one is going to listen to a bunch of kids with sketchy pasts. As fucked up as it is, there's a level of evil brilliance to it."

"Yeah, real fucking genius," Dylan said, reaching down to grab her pack. "Stay put. I'll be back."

"I thought you said you wanted to wait until it got dark?" I said.

But Dylan was already out the door. Jilly replaced the chair behind the doorknob and returned to the sofa beside me, asking, "Do you think she'll be back?"

Honestly, I didn't know. Dylan was a wild card. I could easily see her walking away from us as returning. There was nothing predictable about Dylan. All I could say was, "I hope so" because that was the truth. I didn't like Dylan but we needed her.

Which made it feel as if our survival was tied to a snarling demon who'd just as easily slit our throats as attack our enemy.

I exhaled and closed my eyes. I didn't want to think anymore.

Jilly followed my lead and snuggled against me, whispering with more confidence than I felt, "She'll be back" and I could only hope that Jilly was right.

3

Dylan returned to the church sometime during the night when we were both asleep. I heard the soft knock at the blockaded door and after Dylan identified herself, I let her in.

She didn't say anything, just found a spot to curl up with a blanket and fell instantly asleep.

The next morning we packed up, locked the car with the rest of our stuff, and hit the subway. Dylan wasn't in a chatty mood — not that she ever was — but there was an extra edge to her disposition that made me nervous.

"Where are we going?" I asked, following Dylan down a darkened stairwell that pulled us deeper underground, the sound of the city above us slowly becoming muffled and distant. Urban graffiti covered the cement walls displaying colorful commentary on anything from corruption, gang wars, to incredible artwork splashed in defiant paint across the platform.

My skin puckered with goosebumps beneath my hoodie as the subterranean chill tap-danced on my bones.

Dylan, our foul-mouthed and brusque guide, didn't answer, just motioned for us to follow and to be quiet.

Secrets lurked in the shadows from past and present, whispering of an era when the subway was new and created with the promise of cutting edge technology. Time and neglect had eaten away at the former grandeur of the abandoned station, turning a once-grand dame into a wizened old lady covered in battle scars.

But this place teemed with renegade life from young to ancient. People huddled around burning barrels for heat, wrapped in ragged blankets and covered from head to toe with mismatched articles of clothing, trying to stay warm.

I'd lived in New York most of my life. I knew the stories of the abandoned subway stations but I never realized how an entire segment of society made their way down here to carve out a space of their own amongst the refuse. I was out of my element but Dylan looked right at home.

What kind of rabbit hole had we slid down?

Jilly crowded me, unnerved by the dank oppressive air in the cement tome. "It's like a graveyard for subway trains," she murmured with a mixture of awe and fear. "Who lives here?"

"Aside from sewer rats and killer clowns? No clue," I whispered out of the side of my mouth.

Dylan answered, "His name is Badger and he runs The Runaway Club. You gotta have Badger's permission to be down here or else you're gonna disappear and ain't no one gonna find your corpse."

"Sounds like a great guy," I muttered. "And you know him how?"

"Let's just say we have a history."

Jilly trailed behind Dylan, asking with worry, "Is it a good history?"

"Depends on how he remembers it," Dylan said. "I guess we'll see."

"Hold up," I tugged on Dylan's sleeve, causing Dylan to turn with annoyance. "I thought you said we'd be *safe* here?"

"We will be...if he allows us to stay...and if he doesn't hold a grudge."

Fuuuuuck. "Damn it, Dylan—"

She jerked her arm out of my grasp, her voice a harsh hush, "Look, we're screwed topside anyway so what difference does it make? We take our chances either way. I happen to think we have slightly better odds with Badger than Madame Moirai so shut up and keep walking. Not everyone down here is friendly and you're drawing too much attention."

That was some cockeyed logic but what could I say? Dylan was right. Our lives rested on the edge of a knife's blade and no matter which way we fell, it was going to cut. I could only hope this Badger was the lesser of two evils.

Good-fucking-God, why couldn't anything be easy for once? I didn't want to die in the bowels of a forgotten subway tunnel nor did I want to be chased down like a dog by Madame Moirai and her Avalon squad. I didn't have a choice but to follow Dylan and hope for a fucking miracle.

As my gran would say, "In for a penny, in for a pound."

Dylan rounded the corner and pushed open a heavy steel door that led to a large space illuminated by an orange-tinted light, giving everything an antique look. A forgotten railway car sat among the broken and haphazard remnants of a former life, resting where it'd died, its faded bones still clinging to its identity. Bright light blazed in the car along with the distinct sound of...*classical* music and I was officially bewildered.

She sighed, explaining quickly, "Badger has eclectic tastes." But she tacked on with all seriousness, "If he asks, you prefer Tchaikovsky over Mozart and you think Beethoven is an overrated hack. And do *not* even mention Vivaldi. On second thought, don't say anything."

All I could do was nod. Nothing made sense down here.

As we got closer, I realized the railway car had been turned into a residence and it was definitely occupied.

Two teenage thugs with hard eyes and jaded souls blocked our entrance to the railcar. Dylan scowled. "Get the fuck out of my way, Roach. I need to talk to Badger."

"You've got balls of steel showing your face down here," the one on the right said without budging. "You know there's a bounty on your head?"

"It's nice to be wanted," Dylan said, not the least bit cowed. "Move before I make you regret ever leaving that group home in the Bronx."

"Still the salty bitch," Roach said with a smirk. "I'll laugh when Badger throws your ass into the pit."

I didn't like the sound of that. Jilly and I shared anxious glances as we waited for which way the wheel was going to turn on this fucked up scenario.

"What say you, boss?" he called out.

A long pause followed. Sweat beaded my hairline despite the chill. Dylan held her ground. If she was scared, she didn't show it but I was about to shit my pants. Jilly looked ready to faint.

A tall, lanky 20-something man with a shaved head, worn leathers, and a vivid pink mohawk appeared at the entrance, grabbing onto the poles, a sardonic but hard smile on his face. "Well, look what the cat dragged in," he drawled, using the poles to lean forward menacingly. "I never expected to see your face again. I figured you were smarter than that."

"No one's ever accused me of being smart. I was your No. 1 once, remember? I'd say that was probably the dumbest move of my life."

My eyes bugged. What did that mean? His No. 1?

Badger chuckled, considering his next move. The thick tension in the air coiled around us like a noxious fog but Dylan didn't shake or drop eye contact. The stakes were high in this game and Dylan came to win or lose big.

Which was all well and good, except she brought us along for the game with front row tickets to the sudden death championship and I didn't agree with her choice of entertainment.

"What to do with you..." Badger said, dropping down the steps as his thugs parted to make room. He stood before Dylan, towering over her. "Protocol dictates I should toss you down into the pit."

"But you won't."

Badger held Dylan's gaze as he asked softly, "And why won't I?"

Dylan stared. For a brief moment, it almost seemed as if Dylan were struggling but not with fear. She exhaled a shaky breath, saying, "Because I know who took Nova."

Everything changed in a heartbeat. I stared in confusion. Who the hell was Nova? What the hell was happening? My gaze darted from Dylan to Badger, trying to figure out why they both looked stricken.

Badger stiffened. "What the fuck are you talking about?"

Either Dylan was totally bullshitting to save our asses or there were things Dylan hadn't shared about how she ended up signing with Madame Moirai.

Important things.

My head was spinning. Jilly was just as stunned. Wisely, we kept our mouths shut, too afraid to say anything.

"Don't lie to me," Badger warned, crowding Dylan's personal space. "You better start talking real quick."

But Dylan pushed Badger out of her space with a glower. "Shut up and listen. Nova signed a deal worth a lot of money with a woman named Madame Moirai. She wouldn't give me details but she made me promise not to tell you, saying it was all going to be worth it in the end. I was supposed to pick her up in five days when it was all done but she never showed up and her phone kept going straight to voicemail. When a week went by and she still hadn't contacted me, I knew something had gone wrong."

"What do you mean, gone wrong?"

"You know Nova would never be without her phone," Dylan said, searching his gaze. "If she wasn't answering, something bad had to have gone down. I tried to find her but it was like she disappeared off the face of the planet. I almost gave up. Then, I got a call from an unidentified number, claiming to be an emissary for this Madame Moirai. It was the only lead I had. I had to take it. I had no idea what was going to happen next."

Badger's bewilderment was almost palpable. "I don't understand. Are you telling me someone shook Nova down? Why wouldn't she tell me?"

"There are a lot of things she never told you, Badger. You wouldn't have let her go if you knew and she was determined to make it happen," Dylan said. To my added shock, Dylan's eyes started to water as she said with a catch in her voice, "And knowing what I know now...I wish I had stopped her. It was all a scam. The big pay-out was bullshit."

Badger paled, like someone had just kicked him in the nuts with a steel-toed boot, lodging a vicious ache in his gut. "Where's Nova?"

Dylan looked Badger straight in the eye and answered with undisguised anguish, "I'm pretty sure she's dead." Dylan gestured to me. "If it weren't for her...I'd be dead, too."

I didn't know what to say but I confirmed Dylan's statement with a small nod.

For a long minute, Badger stood, uncomprehending, unable to accept what Dylan had shared but then something must've resonated with his private fears as the words resonated with truth. He dropped to a crouch, a ball of grief and anger, with a roar that I felt in my soul. Dylan dropped to the ground and held him with a ferocity that'd never seen.

Whoever this Nova was, Badger and Dylan had both loved her.

Holy fucking shit.

With sudden clarity, I saw a brand new version of the woman who didn't seem to give a damn about anything or anyone but had a whole lot of fucking secrets locked behind that sharp mouth.

Tana wasn't the only one who'd never left Madame Moirai's care. The sheer scope of what we were staring down was even more overwhelming than before.

And just like that, without realizing the game was open to more players, another piece had been added to the board.

·

4

Alice in Wonderland had nothing on the rabbit hole we were tumbling down in Badger's world. Badger owned a seedy nightclub with a secret entrance into the subway system below where he held court.

Because, only in New York could a street rat punk own real estate without anyone blinking an eye, right?

We followed Badger into a small apartment above the club that smelled like whiskey, stale cigarettes, and bad decisions but at least it wasn't a hollowed-out church slated for demolition.

"What the fuck," Badger shouted once we were inside. His nostrils flared as he demanded, "I want names and I want them now."

"Don't you think if I had names I'd give them to

you?" Dylan said. "All I have is a fucked up situation where I barely got out alive and you."

Badger shoved his hand through his pink faux hawk, pissed as fuck at Dylan's answer, impotent rage in every agitated movement. "I want to know every goddamn detail," he said, pointing at each of us. "I want to know how this all happened and I want to know how the fuck they're getting away with it."

He leveled a stubbed finger at Dylan, saying in a low tone, "Starting with you, baby girl. Start talking."

I held my breath. Dylan hadn't shared any details with us. We had no idea how Dylan had ended up with Madame Moirai and now that we knew Dylan had taken the deal in an attempt to find whoever Nova was...the plot had just thickened to the point of sludge.

"I need a fucking cigarette and a shot," Dylan muttered, accepting a smoke from Badger before crossing to the messy kitchen and finding a bottle of tequila. She didn't bother with a glass. After a quick swig, she winced as it went down and then lit the cigarette, taking a long drag before starting. "I don't know how they found Nova but the best I can figure out is that Nova listed me as her contact on the form, which is how they came looking for me. They made an assessment on me as a risk and decided I fit the criteria for the auction. They killed two birds with one stone — one, they'd remove me as a loose end to Nova and two, they'd make a little money off my sale."

"Sale? What the fuck? What do you mean?"

Dylan took another swig before answering in a dead-pan tone. "We were selling our fucking virginities to rich perverts. That's the deal we were offered. Sixty percent of any transaction would supposedly go to us whereas Madame Moirai would take forty. Seeing as each sale could potentially go for hundreds of thousands, our cut seemed more than generous. The money is the bait and it fucking worked."

"Why wouldn't Nova tell me this?" Badger asked.

"Because you're a dick at best and at worst, her brother. Like you were going to be chill with her selling herself? You never wanted that for Nova. Not on the streets, not for some rich asshole."

"And she fucking sold herself anyway..." Badger looked ready to punch something or throw up — maybe both. "So...okay, what happened after the sale?"

"We were taken back to the place where we were being held and then...well, I can only assume that they were going to overdose us and then get rid of our bodies."

"What makes you think that?" Badger asked, trying to piece together the story. "Why not just keep you on your backs for more money?"

His blunt question made me wince, reminding me of Olivia's offer to elevate. I chimed in. "If you were offered to elevate, that's exactly what would've happened but not everyone is given that offer. Out of the four of us...I was the only one offered."

"Four?" Badger's gaze darted between us. "I only see three of you."

"One of us died," I answered, swallowing the bile in my throat. "Her name was Tana. I found her body downstairs in a make-shift morgue. It looked like they were going to embalm her or something."

Badger's expression screwed into a frown. "What the fuck does elevate mean?"

"It means you remain in service to your buyer," I answered, feeling sick. "If they want more, they make an offer to keep you. I told my handler, I'd rather fucking die."

"What if Nova was, like you said, *elevated*?" Badger supposed, thinking out loud. "You never saw Nova's body, right?"

"No," Dylan admitted. "But my gut says she's gone."

"You ain't psychic," Badger reminded Dylan with a hard look. "My sister could still be alive."

"Maybe," I agreed but I had to be honest with him even if he was terrifying. "My handler said that an offer of elevation is rare. The odds aren't good."

"Yeah, well Nova was special," Badger said with a glower as I'd insulted his sister just by sharing the truth. I zipped my lip after that. Badger had the irrational energy of someone marinating in extreme grief and I wasn't about to mess with that.

"Nova was special," Dylan agreed, her gaze downcast. "She didn't deserve this shit." She looked up, pining Badger's stare. "None deserves what they're doing to innocent girls."

A silent, unspoken conversation flowed between Badger and Dylan. After a long, tense moment, Badger looked away, going to drop into a misshapen recliner, rubbing his forehead. "Fuck," he said, the single word heavy with grief and rage. "I can't believe this shit."

"It's a nightmare," Dylan agreed, returning to fall into the sofa beside us. "There's some kind of network...The Avalon or something like that. Pretty fucking powerful. They've got connections in all sorts of places. I don't know what to do."

Badger's gaze roamed our faces, realizing we might have intel worth listening to. He looked to me and Jilly. "You all were virgins?"

My cheeks heated. "Yeah."

"So some rich asshole popped your cherry and then ran out on the bill," Badger said, summing up the experience. As if that short, terse statement could possibly wrap up the horrid details of everything we'd been through.

I gritted my teeth, not trusting my mouth. Instead, I jerked a short nod. Dylan could feel my temper building. She interjected, saying, "Look, if it weren't Nicole, I wouldn't be here. She's a fucking savage. She jimmied the locks to our rooms and then set fire to the place where they were holding us. We're alive because of this chick right here."

Grudging respect lifted the corner of his mouth. "Yeah? Tell me how you managed that."

"Picking locks isn't that hard if you've got the right tools. I found a bobby pin in the carpet. The locks were simple. I waited until after midnight when I was sure the staff was at its lowest and then I opened the other doors."

"They kept you in separate rooms?" Badger asked, intrigued.

Dylan answered for me, bitterness coating her tone. "Yeah, like prison cells with a Best Western hotel vibe. We were locked in every night and fed this disgusting paste that was supposed to be oatmeal. It was pretty clear they didn't give two shits about our comfort after we'd been returned. We didn't even get any medical care for our bodies after we'd been beaten and abused."

Badger's gaze narrowed. "Show me."

Dylan didn't flinch, just lifted her shirt to show the mottled bruising riddling her ribcage, traveling down her belly and disappearing behind her jeans. We all had bruises. Dylan had broken bones, too. "They didn't pay just for the privilege of fucking virgins," she said, her voice clogged. "They paid to do whatever the fuck they wanted."

I closed my eyes as the memory of Tana's broken body flashed in my mind. "Tana was beaten to death," I said. "We don't know if she died at the house or with her buyer but she died of her injuries."

"Nicole found her body," Dylan explained, shifting against the heaviness in the room. Each time we talked about Tana, I felt the energy of her ghost lurking in the shadows. "She was pretty fucked up."

Badger processed our answers and I knew he was replacing Tana with his Nova, knowing that she probably suffered before dying, too. That red-hot rage returned and I didn't blame him but he was as unpredictable as Dylan. I didn't know if we were safe with him but I knew we weren't safe out there in the open.

We had to take our chances with Badger.

"I want names," Badger repeated, his gaze hard and brittle. "Someone needs to pay for what they did to Nova." He silenced Dylan with a look when she started to protest. "I.Want.Names."

The tense stand-off between the two held the air in our lungs with an iron-grip. I couldn't breathe, afraid to tip the scales in any way against us. Badger was the key to surviving with Madame Moirai on our heels.

And Dylan was our negotiator.

Just when the tension felt ready to break, Dylan leaned forward with a hard look of her own, saying, "If you want names, you're going to have to help us. Call in your favors. We're going to need all of them. If you're not willing to do that, you don't really want to know what happened to Nova and you sure as hell don't want to avenge her."

Dylan had thrown the gauntlet but what else

could she do in light of the circumstances. We didn't have a snowball's chance in hell of finding out jack shit without some kind of help. If Badger had resources, he had to pony up if he wanted results.

Badger's mouth turned up, conceding Dylan's point without saying a word. He looked to Jilly and me, gesturing, "And these two?"

"They're with me."

It was the first real indication Dylan wasn't going anywhere, that she wasn't going to ditch us at the first chance.

"There's rules," Badger reminded Dylan. I wanted to know what these rules were and if they involved this infamous pit for breaking them. I didn't run from sexual slavery only to land in a pit of some kind in the bowels of New York. "You responsible for them?"

"Yeah," Dylan answered, sealing some kind of unspoken agreement for us. "You gonna help?"

Badger inhaled a deep breath, considering his position. He had loved his sister, but was he willing to put everything on the line to bring down the people responsible for her death? This could all go sidewise, real quick and he seemed slick enough to recognize the threat.

Finally, he nodded. "Yeah, I'll help. I've got some

people I can call up but these two," he pointed to me and Jilly "they're gonna have to make themselves useful. There ain't no free ride. Not even for Nova. Everyone pitches in. You remember."

"Yeah, I remember." Dylan didn't like the terms but we were all up against a rock and a hard place. She countered, saying, "Any job you're thinking of running with them, you check with me first. They don't know what the hell they're doing and I'm not taking the heat for their stupidity."

Was that a backhanded attempt at protecting us? I grit my teeth against the need to tell her to fuck off. I wasn't fragile or easily scared off and like I mentioned, I was pretty sure Jilly had a screw loose. I think we could handle ourselves.

But this was Dylan's world and I didn't know the rules yet. I had to keep quiet, watch and learn.

Felt a lot like surviving my fucking childhood.

5

Badger left us behind in the apartment. Once he was gone, Jilly announced, "Well he seems nice," to which Dylan countered with an eye roll that said the opposite.

I regarded Dylan, too many questions vying for time in my mouth. "Is everything you said about Nova the truth?"

"Why the fuck would I lie about that?" Dylan shot back, rubbing at her eyes. Now that Badger was gone she seemed to break down a little, like she had to hold herself together so as not to show any weakness around him. "Nova was my best and only friend. I loved her."

"Why didn't you say something about your

friend from the start?" I asked, bewildered. "I don't understand why you kept that quiet."

"Because I had no reason to trust you and it was my business."

I suppose that was fair but for some reason, I felt betrayed that she hadn't been upfront about how she came to be an auction girl. But that information changed things a bit. If Madame Moirai selected Dylan because she was on Nova's contact sheet, that meant they'd deliberately target Dylan. I shuddered at how close I'd been to putting Lora's name down as my contact. I couldn't handle the idea of Lora going through what we had. It would've been a death sentence for Lora just as it had been for Tana and however many other girls who'd been baited and trapped.

"How did you meet Badger and Nova?" I asked.

"Nova found me on the street. She introduced me to Badger, said I couldn't survive without someone to look out for me. She introduced me to Badger and I started running jobs for him in exchange for protection. We got close. All of us. Before too long, I was Badger's No. 1 runner. Gained a reputation for getting jobs done without drawing attention to myself. Badger liked that about me."

"Was there ever a thing between you and Badger?" I asked.

"Fuck no. Badger has a strict no-messing-around policy with his runners, says it fucks up the chain of command. I can't say he's wrong. Besides, he's like a brother to me."

I've never had a sibling but having a brother like Badger? Not sure that was a great endorsement. "So, why didn't Nova tell Badger about Madame Moirai?"

"Badger is like most big brothers — overprotective, belligerent and most the time he just didn't listen to a thing Nova had to say if it didn't jive with what he wanted her to say." Dylan paused, reflecting, "And I don't know, I think she was looking for an opportunity to do her own thing. Badger is a control freak, even with the ones he loves. He doesn't trust easily and if you happen to betray that trust, you're going to end up in the fucking pit."

There was the mention of that pit again. "What the hell is that?"

Dylan smirked. "Let's just say if you end up in the pit you ain't never coming back."

I guess that's all I needed to know. I didn't have any plans to land in any kind of pit. "I'm sorry about your friend," I said quietly.

Jilly piped in. "Yeah, that's so terrible. She must've been real special. I'm sorry."

Dylan shrugged with a *whatever* energy but I knew it was fake. Even Dylan knew the agony of heartbreak. For the sake of her pride, I changed the subject. "What kind of contacts does Badger have? Does he really have someone who can help us find more about The Avalon network?"

"Badger knows people in all places. He's probably the most dangerous person nobody knows about. He keeps it that way for a reason. But yeah he's got contacts. We just need to lay low until he tells us what and who we should talk to."

Jilly asked, "What kind of jobs does he want us to do? I'm a little confused. We're not old enough to work in the club downstairs, right?"

Dylan answered wryly. "Nothing so visible. Badger runs this town. He runs anything from drugs to guns, pretty much anything and everything that is for sale except he doesn't traffic in people. That's the one line he won't cross. Anything else is fair game. Basically, if he gives you a job here as a runner, the best advice I can give you is if he gives you a job, do as you're told, don't ask questions and don't screw up. If you do that you'll be fine but I'm gonna try to keep you out of the runner circle."

I asked, "How do you suppose to manage that? I mean I know you and Badger have history or something but he doesn't seem all that lenient or open to suggestion."

"Don't worry. I'll handle Badger. You just do what you can to get answers because we're on the line."

"What happens if we can't find answers?" I asked.

I could tell by Dylan's expression that wasn't an option. Even if Badger had some kind of soft feelings for Dylan he wasn't going to let feelings get in the way of his revenge. And if there wasn't someone to pay for what had happened to Nova, we would pay instead.

It was one thing to think you were tough because you lived in a rough area of the city but quite another when the sharp edge of society is pressed against your throat. One wrong move and you're fucked.

I hope we hadn't jumped from the frying pan to the fire.

"Badger said we can hole up here for the time being," Dylan said. "At least it's not down below with the sewer rats."

I shuddered, glancing around. "Does Badger live here?"

"Sometimes. It depends on the day. He's got places all over the city. He likes to have options."

I bit my lip, wondering if I should ask but I did anyway. The way Dylan appeared uncomfortable and yet familiar with the apartment made me wonder. "Did you live here with Nova?"

"Yeah," she admitted, gesturing, "We shared that room."

"Are you going to be okay staying here?" I asked.

"I'll be fine," Dylan said but she looked as if that room was filled with poison. She dragged her gaze away from that direction, saying, "Look, now that Badger has given us the green light to crash here, we need to get our stuff and ditch the car."

I agreed. We still had supplies, extra clothes and food stashed in the car behind the church. If we waited too long, it would all be gone.

Jilly volunteered, raising her hand. "I'll go with you. I need some fresh air."

Dylan nodded. "Let's go. I want to get this over with." To me, she said, "Don't leave. We'll be back soon."

"Bring back a pizza," I said, settling onto the lumpy couch, happy to stay behind. I could only handle so much of Dylan and to be honest, a little alone time sounded perfect. I wasn't much of a people person on my best day, much less under the circumstances and both Dylan and Jilly's personalities were a bit much.

The girls left me behind and I closed my eyes with a long exhale. Except I always saw Tana's body when I tried to sleep. My eyes popped open, regardless of the grit of sleep deprivation and the sheer mental exhaustion sucking the life out of me.

I must've dozed for a little while. I woke with a start to hear the front door opening and Badger returning. He carried a bag of groceries, which seemed an odd thing to see in his arms. I know people have to eat but I never imagined someone like Badger walking the aisles of a local bodega for pantry items.

"You like spaghetti?" he asked, pulling items from the bag. He didn't wait for my answer, saying, "Well, it's for dinner so you'd better like it because I ain't running no restaurant."

"I like most food," I answered, rising to walk over to the kitchen. "Need help?"

He pushed the vegetables my way. "You can start chopping. I like a salad with pasta. Have you ever noticed that when you're poor, fresh produce is like rich people food? It's tough to eat healthy when you ain't got shit. Cheaper to eat garbage than anything good for you." He pointed an old wooden spoon at me. "That's the government making sure that the poor people stay sick so they can experiment on you with their weird-ass shit. I kid you not, true story. Don't ask me how I know."

I knew a smile wasn't the right response but Badger's conspiracy theories were just the right amount of crazy to lighten the mood, even if he hadn't meant to.

"You think I sound crazy, right?" he said, reading my mind. "That's okay, you just don't know. You're ignorant but stick with me and I'll educate you."

I wasn't sticking around to become Badger's protege but he didn't need to know that. "Thanks for helping us out. I'm sorry about Nova."

"Yeah, she was a good kid," he said, avoiding eye contact as he started mincing garlic. He switched subjects as if he couldn't talk about Nova. "The thing is, a good sauce has to have plenty of garlic. Everybody knows that but it also takes time to make sure the sauce has enough marinating time, you know?" Except Nova made her way into his thoughts anyway. Grief had a way of doing that. He shook his head, adding as if annoyed, "Nova was always rushing me. Saying nobody cared about the marinating but I cared. I mean, no sense in doing something unless you do right. Nova was always looking for the shortcut. Damn her little cheating ass. Always about the fucking shortcut."

My cheeks burned. Hadn't we all been looking for the shortcut? A quick route out of the misery of our lives? Guilty as charged.

"I thought she was smarter than that," Badger said, stilling. "She could've gone to college, made something of herself, gotten out of this life and gone legit. *Goddamn it*, Nova."

That last part, muttered with anger, hid a wealth of agony from a big brother who'd probably been watching out for his little sister since they were both small. I didn't know their story but whatever they'd had together had been real.

"You got any siblings?" he asked. I shook my head. He grunted. "You're lucky. All you gotta care about is yourself. Easier that way."

"Lonelier too," I admitted.

"Fuck that. You're only lonely if you let yourself be. Plenty of people to spend your time with in this world. People are a dime a dozen."

I didn't argue. I was living on his dime, in his domain. I wasn't about to strike up a debate about the validity of his claim. Besides, what did I know?

Maybe he was right. Caring about people made you and them vulnerable.

But I missed Lora. I wanted to call her so bad. She was probably worried sick by now.

"Hey, so they took our phones when we got to the place and we never got them back. Do you think you could hook us up with some burners?" I asked, adding, "I got money. I can pay you."

"I can make that happen. Who you want to call?"

I shrugged. "No one. I just don't like being without a phone. Makes me feel vulnerable."

"I got you." He nodded wisely. "Yeah, sure, I'll hook you up. Don't worry about the money. We'll settle up later."

I'd rather pay. I didn't like anyone having something over me. I'd deal with that later. I nodded, seeming to accept his offer. Now was not the time to make waves.

We worked side by side in silence, finishing up the spaghetti. By the time Jilly and Dylan returned, we had a decent meal to put on the rickety table.

Genuine joy spread across Dylan's face as she tucked into the mound of spaghetti. It was probably like the way I felt when I'd walk into my Gran's house, the lingering smell of cigarettes and whatever she was cooking hanging in the air. For me, it always felt like home.

I saw that in Dylan's expression — however, fucked up things were, she was home.

Tears sprang to my eyes. I hid my reaction by focusing on my own plate.

I blamed exhaustion for the pain that burned like a raw, angry bruise on my heart.

Easier than admitting I was homesick, too.

6

I woke the next morning to Dylan and Badger shouting.

"You should've fucking told me what Nova was up to! Maybe if you'd opened your fucking mouth and told me, I could've saved her from making a huge mistake!"

"She asked me not to tell you," Dylan shouted back. "What part of that don't you understand? I was being loyal to my best friend. Besides, how was I supposed to know this was going to happen? Don't you think if I'd known that she was in any danger, I would've stopped her myself? Jesus, Badger, you act like you're the only one who lost her. I loved her, too!"

"Not enough to keep her from getting herself

fucking killed," Badger returned with cold cruelty. "It's your fault she's dead."

I held my breath, shocked. Dylan stared, the pain of his accusation cutting so deep I could feel the agony across my own heart. I had to say something before they destroyed each other. I scrambled to my feet, stepping between them. "Look, it's getting pretty heated. We need to take a step back and calm down. If we start attacking each other, they win. You get it? If we're spending all our time and energy fighting each other, no one is making them pay for what they done. Are you going to do that or are you going to suck it up and work together because let me know now if you're no use to me."

It was a bold fucking move on my part but from what I learned about Dylan was that sometimes she respected you more with savagery. Now that I'd met Badger, it made more sense — and if Dylan was that way, it stood to reason that Badger was the same.

Badger, amused, said, "You think you can do this on your own?"

"Maybe. Maybe not but if you're not going to be useful, then I don't really have a choice, do I? You weren't there when I was jimmying the locks in the dead of night while locked away in Madame Moirai's mansion, were you? I got myself out of that place. I'll find a way to make them pay on my own if I have to."

I meant every word. There was a part of me that was stone-cold savage and if I had to tap into that place, I would. No one, not even Badger and his underground Runaway Club of vicious misfits would stop me.

"Your sister kept you out of the loop. It was part of our agreement we made with Madame Moirai. They made it sound like we were being watched from the moment we signed the contract. She probably didn't want to blow her shot so she didn't say anything to anyone but Dylan and then made Dylan promise to keep quiet because, for all she knew, any breach of the contract would cost her the money. That's what they do — they use our desperate need for money to make us do stupid shit. Trust me, I feel sick to my stomach for being duped so easily but here we are. You beating Dylan over the head over a mistake we all made isn't going to get us anywhere so shut the fuck up already. I have a headache from sleeping on the couch and I haven't had any coffee yet. Got it?"

Dylan looked apprehensive and impressed at the same time. I probably just earned myself a one-way ticket to this infamous "pit" but I didn't have the patience to tip-toe around drama that we couldn't afford. There was a group of sociopaths after us with unlimited resources. Now wasn't the time to jerk around with bullshit blame.

"I feel you," Badger said, gazing at me with something more akin to respect. To Dylan, he said, "Fine, we'll table this discussion until a later date."

"Oh goody, something to look forward to," Dylan countered sourly. "I'm with Nicole, let's get the coffee started before I murder someone for looking at me funny."

"Nice to see some things don't change," Badger said, moving to the kitchen to start the coffee in the old coffee maker. He looked to me. "Straight black or creamer?"

"You got creamer?"

"I wouldn't ask if I didn't."

"Then yeah, I like creamer, the sweeter the better."

Jilly appeared, yawning, scratching her behind. "Jesus, you guys are fucking loud. What are you yelling about?" Before anyone could answer, she waved away our response, disinterested. "Forget it, never mind. Just pour the coffee. That's all I care about for the moment."

Crisis averted. At least for now. Once we all had

a cup, I returned to the topic that mattered. "Do you know any cops or anything who can help us get information on The Avalon or Madame Moirai?"

"Maybe. First, give me the run-down of this operation. I want to know how it all came together." He gestured to me. "Starting with you."

"My story is about the same as all of ours. Someone approached me on behalf of someone named Madame Moirai. They offered me a lot of money for my virginity and I took it. We had a set of rules we had to follow before the pick-up and then a car came and picked me up bringing me to the mansion. At first, I thought it was pretty fancy and that maybe this was really an up and up deal for rich weirdos with fucked up fetishes or something but then I got locked into a big room with four beds. That's when I met Dylan, Jilly, and Tana."

"Tana's the dead one?" Badger asked.

I narrowed my gaze at his insensitive tone. "Yeah. She's the one who died. Like Nova," I added without mercy.

Badger's nostrils flared but he didn't counter or retaliate.

I continued. "We were prepared for the auction—"

"Prepared? What do you mean?"

Dylan interjected, irritated. "She means we were plucked, prodded and given enemas so that we were primed and ready in case some sick fucker wanted to shove their dicks up our ass."

"Did they?" Badger asked.

"Fuck you," Dylan muttered.

But I held Badger's gaze. If he wanted to know the gory details, so be it. "Yeah, and it was awful, degrading and painful. Then, after he'd violated my ass, he beat me until I cried for mercy. It's a miracle he didn't break any bones." I shared a look with Dylan, returning to Badger. "Not everyone was so lucky. Tana was broken into pieces by the time they finished with her. That satisfy your curiosity?"

"Fuck, that's messed up," Badger said, his voice subdued.

The blood had left Jilly's face. Not even the heat from the mug of coffee could pinken those cheeks. She'd never shared what her buyer had done to her. I assumed it was horrific. I didn't need details. Then, she looked up and shared, "Nicole knows her buyer's name."

"Serious?" Badger asked.

"Yeah. A French man named Henri Benoit."

"Why did he tell you his name?" Badger asked,

regarding me open speculation. "Seems like a stupid thing to do."

"At first arrogance, I guess. He must've known that Madame Moirai disposes of her auction girls at the end but then he made an offer to elevate so he probably thought I was coming back to him."

"Elevate...pretty fancy word for a sex slave," Badger figured out. "What made him think you'd be open to being with him again after he'd fucked you up?"

"How the fuck should I know?" I snapped. "It's not like we ended the night holding hands and whispering sweet fucking nothings in each other's ears. By the time I left his place, all I wanted to do was escape, get paid and forget it ever happened."

"So, by my calculation, you're owed some money..." Badger said.

"Yeah, about sixty or seventy grand," I said.

He looked to Dylan and Jilly, motioning, "Same for you, two?"

"About the same," Dylan answered.

"Now that's something I understand. Services rendered, money paid. That's how these things work."

"Not to mention what was owed Nova," I

reminded him, holding his stare. "If Nova's gone, that would make you the next of kin, right?"

Badger leaned back, his eyes glittering with the new angle. "That's about right, indeed."

It wasn't about the money but if the money helped grease the wheels more effectively than pure sentiment and emotion, so be it.

"I know a guy who might be able to help. Ex-cop turned P.I. He does some work for me from time to time. Stuff that needs to keep quiet. I can trust him."

"What's his name?"

"Adrian Hicks."

Dylan said, "Never heard of him."

"Your point?" Badger countered.

"I'm just saying I know all your contacts and I've never heard you mention anyone named Hicks."

"Don't be so full of yourself, bitch. I got contacts you ain't never heard of and you never will. You want the help or not?"

Dylan flipped Badger off and returned to her coffee in sullen silence. I was starting to realize this was their relationship: surly, adversarial and yet oddly protective. *Talk about dysfunction.* Something I recognized well.

Badger pushed off the counter to reach into a drawer, pulling three phones free. "Burners with hacked SIMS. Unlimited calls. Only I have the numbers. Keep it that way. If I call, make sure you answer."

I reached over and grabbed a phone as Jilly and Dylan did the same. I murmured my thanks, catching a quick look from Dylan. Losing our phones was just another violation of our dignity to add to the list. What I hated more was that they had access to our lives through our contacts, pictures, videos and even the apps we used.

Anything they wanted to know about us, could be found in those phones. With any luck, our phones burned in the fire I set.

"When can we meet this Hicks?" I asked.

"I'll make some calls. I'll let you know." He looked to Dylan. "You up for a job while you wait?"

She seemed to anticipate his offer, agreeing with a shrug. "Anything to get out of the apartment."

"Good."

As much as they bickered and seemed to purposefully stab each other when they could, Badger understood she couldn't stay cooped inside an apartment with Nova's ghost. I would feel the same if I was mourning Lora.

Speaking of. I needed to talk to her. If our phones weren't destroyed in the fire, I needed to make sure Lora was okay. Also, I didn't want her to worry.

With Dylan out of the house, I could sneak away and make a call. I knew it was risky and probably stupid but I was going to do it anyway.

If anything, I needed something to remind me of before this all happened, before Henri Benoit had stained my soul forever with his nasty touch.

Before I'd foolishly sold something before knowing it's true value.

Hell, maybe I just wanted to pretend for a second that everything was fine, life was normal and all I needed to worry about was a chem test.

Because that wasn't my reality.

Our reality was much darker.

We were as good as dead if the wrong people found us before we could find a way to save our skins.

I didn't want to die.

I blinked back tears.

I was still just a kid.

Why the hell didn't I feel like one anymore?

7

Jilly left with Dylan after Badger skipped out for the day, leaving me alone. I showered and dressed quickly, grabbed the burner phone and headed out.

On the subway to Manhattan, I called Lora. Thankfully, I knew her number, one of the few I knew by heart, and held my breath waiting for her to answer.

I wasn't surprised when the first call went to voicemail. No one picked up an unknown number on the first ring. I left a quick message, letting her know it was me and that I would call right back.

On the first ring of the second call, Lora's voice was in my ear.

"Oh my God, Nicole! Where the fuck are you?

Where have you been? Seriously, oh my God! Are you okay?"

"I will tell you everything but not on the phone. Can you get away and meet me at The Cruller? I'll be there in about thirty minutes."

The Cruller was a favorite bakery of ours with the most amazing pastries in the city. Lora and I used to make the trip to Crullers at least once a month to celebrate whatever victories we'd accomplished. It was Lora's idea and I wasn't about to turn down the opportunity to eat pastries so I agreed. After that, it just evolved into our own little ritual and I missed it.

"How am I supposed to ditch school and get to the city before my mom finds out I'm gone? Why can't you just come to my place?"

Impatience laced my tone. "Lora, find a fucking way, okay? I can't come to your place. It's safer to meet in public away from your house."

"Safer? What do you mean? Are you in some kind of trouble? If you are we should tell my dad. He can help."

"For God's sake Lora, just listen to me. This isn't something your dad can handle and I wouldn't involve him or you anyway. Can you meet me or not?"

"I guess but it won't be easy."

Her reluctance hurt my feelings. "Forget it, then," I said, tears stinging my eyes.

"Hold your horses, Jesus, I'm coming I'm just saying, it's going to be a bitch trying to get there and back without freaking out my parents. I'll see you in thirty."

I clicked off and wiped at my eyes. I'd always known that Lora was a little spoiled but never had it become so apparent that we were from different worlds than now when I needed her most.

Contacting her was a mistake. Maybe I shouldn't go. But even as I knew it was probably the best way to remedy this situation, I couldn't ghost my best friend. It wasn't her fault that she'd been raised in a loving home with normal, boring parents and I hadn't.

Was I really going to tell Lora what happened to me? What I'd agreed to and how I'd ended up on the run? I'd have to if any of this was going to make sense to her. Otherwise, she'd just do something stupid like go to the cops in some misguided attempt at helping, which I couldn't afford.

I walked into Crullers, the familiar, comforting smell of dough, sugar and warm air, caressed my soul in a way that nearly buckled my knees. I ordered two fresh crullers and two hot chocolates, our standing order, and waited.

Just when I thought Lora had bailed on me, she walked into the bakery, searching for me among the patrons. Her eyes lit up with genuine relief as she hustled over to me, sliding into the booth, reaching for my hand to squeeze it in hers. "Are you okay?" was her first question, followed immediately by "You have no idea how out of my mind I've been. You've got some explaining to do."

I smiled, my throat closing as I nodded. I gestured to the cruller. "I got our favorite."

"Not that I don't love a good cruller but I need to know what the hell is going on, Nicole."

The subtle admonishment in her tone landed like an anvil on my shoulders. It was either now or never if I was going to be honest about what had happened. *Here goes nothing...*

"Listen to me, what I'm about to tell you is going to upset you but I need you to promise me that you'll keep your mouth shut, okay?"

Lora's brow furrowed in confusion. "I'm sure whatever you did is fixable—"

"Stop. It's not that simple and the fix is anything but easy. Just promise me you'll listen without judgment and that you'll keep it to yourself. You can't even tell your parents, okay?"

"That's a pretty tall order," she admitted, biting her lip. "And you're kinda scaring me. You've been gone for almost two weeks. That's serious. I mean, you're truant now. I think that goes on your school record. How's that going to look on your transcripts?"

Transcripts? Jesus, college was the last thing on my mind. "Shut up and listen, okay?" I said, almost begging her to zip her trap. "I will tell you everything but for God's sake, shut up already. What I'm dealing with is far more serious than being truant."

Lora blinked in shock as I'd no doubt hurt her feelings but I didn't have time to coddle her. Was this what I always did with Lora? Coddled her for the sake of keeping the peace or protecting her?

"Fine. Okay, say what you have to say," Lora said, slumping against the booth with a subtle petulance that was hard to miss, adding with a sniff, "But you don't have to be rude about it."

"Sorry," I mumbled "but I...never mind. Here's the deal...the reason I'm meeting with you is because you might be in danger because of a deal I made with some shady people. I just want to be sure that you're safe."

"What do you mean? Are you into drugs or something?"

"Not drugs. There's no easy way to explain this so I'm going to be blunt: I sold my virginity to some rich perverts that turned out to be shady criminals and now I'm a loose end they can't afford. I don't want you to get caught up in this net so I'm telling you now, don't talk to anyone about me or tell them that you've had contact, okay?"

"Are you freaking kidding me?" she asked, bewildered. "The words that just came out of your mouth make zero sense. I mean, *what*? You sold your...seriously?"

My stomach sunk. What the hell was I thinking telling Lora? She wasn't going to listen to reason. I was stupid to come. I wanted to kick myself for ignoring my gut instincts. *Again.* I tried again, desperately hoping I could pierce through the crust created by her happy and cozy life.

"Lora...I know this is hard for you to grasp but there are really bad people who not only want me dead but need me to be gone to keep their secret. They will stop at nothing to make sure I stay quiet. Get it?"

"Sounds pretty dramatic," Lora said, not understanding. "Why don't you just go to the police if it's that bad?"

"Because people with this kind of money, likely have cops on their payroll, get it?"

"This isn't a movie, Nicole...that doesn't happen in real life," she scoffed, wrinkling her brow with irritation as if I were making all of this up for attention. "Seriously, I doubt it's all that bad. Just go tell the police and they can sort all this out."

Tears stung my eyes. She didn't understand. She never would understand. "Did you hear a word I said?"

"Yes, every word and I'm kinda pissed that you would do something so...disgusting, honestly. You sold your virginity? Like, *gross*. That's something you save for your husband, not some weirdo random stranger."

"Not everyone has a college fund, Lora," I reminded her quietly, my heart hurting too much to trust saying much else. I never realized Lora could be so dense, so lacking in empathy that she would judge me so harshly for a decision that I clearly regretted. I grabbed my backpack. "I'm sorry I came. Look, whether you believe me or not, the threat is real. Don't talk to anyone and forget you ever saw me. As far as you're concerned...I just disappeared."

When Lora realized I was about to bail, she grabbed my arm in alarm. "Wait, I'm sorry...don't go. I just don't understand...I can't wrap my head around what you're telling me and I'm struggling. I'm sorry if I'm not saying the right things. I don't mean to hurt your feelings."

Deep down I'd known this would be Lora's reaction, which was why I hadn't told her in the first place. It wasn't her fault that she couldn't understand. It was my fault for placing that burden on her shoulders. I blinked against the tears stinging my eyes. I leaned down to hug her hard. "Don't talk to anyone, please," I whispered into her ear before letting go, saying, "I'll try to call when I can."

Lora tried protesting but I was out the door and gone before she could chase after me.

My life as I'd known it was as dead as the girl on the slab. There was no coming back after what'd been done to us. At some point, I just had to accept that as fact no matter how much it hurt.

Tears streamed down my face as I ran. I finally stopped, my chest screaming for air as the bitter cold of a New York winter cut into my lungs. I glanced up at the darkened sky. It might snow tonight. I dragged my arm across my face, wiping away the wetness.

My best friend in the world, the only person who

really loved me, thought I was being a drama queen about the most horrific experience of my life.

She didn't believe me when I told her that someone was likely after me and the cops were no help.

All I had in the world was Jilly and Dylan — only because they were in the same position, not because we cared about each other.

I was forced to rely on the kindness of a man I couldn't trust while putting my fate in the hands of strangers who only had my back for as long as it benefitted them in some way.

With those odds, it seemed only a matter of time before I ended up dead. A prickling on the back of my neck caused me to turn and stare behind me. Throngs of people flowed onto the sidewalk. Was someone watching me? Being out in the open made me nervous. Eyes could be everywhere. I had no idea how connected The Avalon network was but I wouldn't put it past them to have eyes in the sky, using the traffic cams and facial recognition technology to find me.

Maybe I was paranoid.

Maybe I wasn't being paranoid enough.

All I knew was that I didn't want to remain on the street much longer.

I ducked down into the subway entrance, feeling only marginally better in the confines of the subterranean transit system but nothing truly settled the feeling that I was being watched.

Only then, sitting by myself, as the blurred cement landscape passed me by, did I let the tears flow. I just said goodbye to my best friend but Lora didn't even realize we'd probably never see each other again.

I'd rationalized that I'd only wanted to make sure she was safe but the real reason was far more selfish — I'd wanted to see someone who knew me before all of this had changed me.

I wanted to see who I'd been through their eyes.

Except...it never works like that, does it?

All I saw was someone I'd left behind.

And my heart broke all over again.

Madame Moirai had stolen far more than my paltry virginity — she'd stolen my future self because I'd never be the same after what she'd done to me.

Ever.

8

Dylan pounced on me the minute I returned to the apartment, eyes blazing with accusation and fear.

"Where the fuck have you been?"

I dropped my pack to the floor, glaring as I shot back, "You're not my fucking warden and I don't have to check in with you, so fuck off."

But Dylan wasn't backing down. She shocked me when she tried grabbing me. I slapped her hand away with a snarl. "Don't fucking touch me," I warned. "Or I will remove that fucking hand. Got it?"

Jilly jumped in, scared. "Guys, don't fight. We were just worried about you, okay?" she said, trying to smooth things over. "We got back to the apartment and you weren't answering your phone. We thought that Madame Moirai had found you, that's all. We're glad you're safe."

Dylan held my stare, hot and angry. If there was some truth to Jilly's statement, Dylan wasn't showing it but I sensed Jilly was probably being honest in ways Dylan couldn't. Dylan wasn't exactly the touchy-feely type. Every emotion funneled back to anger at some point. If she was worried, she'd likely respond with rage because she didn't know how to process anything more complex. I let my anger recede. I understood Dylan more than I wanted to. "I went to talk to my friend Lora. I didn't want her to worry but also, I wanted to warn her not to talk to anyone about me in case Madame Moirai's people started sniffing around."

"You should've told us before you left," Dylan said, still pissed. "How do you know you can trust your friend not to rat you out?"

"Lora's not like that," I said, defending Lora. "She's trustworthy."

"Everyone has a price. If The Avalon starts throwing cash at her, she'll talk."

I hated Dylan being right. Going to see Lora was stupid but I couldn't take it back. "Look, I just wanted to make sure she was okay. She's not like us. She's got a nice family and she's normal. I didn't want anything to come back on her because of what I'd done, okay?"

Jilly nodded, understanding but Dylan was being a bitch. "If anything comes back on *us* because of your stupidity, I'll fucking kill you myself."

"Okay, Bad-Ass," I quipped with enough sarcasm to kill a horse. "Calm yourself. Nothing is going to happen. We met at a small out of the way bakery and then I took the subway back."

"Someone could've seen you and followed you," Dylan said.

"I wasn't followed."

"How do you know?"

"Because I made sure," I said. "I wasn't fucking born yesterday."

Dylan settled a little but grumbled, "Yeah, well, if you keep making dumb-ass decisions like that, makes me wonder."

"I don't need you to police me, Dylan," I told her, going to the kitchen to grab some left-over spaghetti. My sprint had burned up all the calories from my cruller and I was starved. "What's the word on Badger's PI? I want to get moving on some leads. I'm not about to spend my entire life constantly looking over my shoulder. At some point, I want to be able to put all of this behind me."

"You really think that's possible?" Dylan asked, incredulous. "Girl, this shit is tattooed on our souls for the rest of our lives. There ain't no escaping what we've got in our heads."

"I'll find a way as long as I'm not dodging bullets at the same time."

Jilly asked, "Did you have a nice visit with your friend?"

I dug into the cold spaghetti. "Not really," I admitted around a huge bite. "Lora couldn't understand why I just didn't go to the cops."

"Do you think she'll talk?" Jilly asked, worried.

"No," I lied. No sense in admitting I shared the same concern, giving Dylan more to bitch about. "She's cool. I mean, she can't understand what I'm going through but she trusts me enough to believe me when I say it's not safe to talk about me to anyone."

Dylan shook her head, still thinking I was stupid for talking to my friend. I ignored Dylan as I continued to eat. Jilly sat on the sofa, drawing her knees to her chest, saying wistfully, "I'm jealous that you have someone who still cares about you in the real world. I never really had many connections to hold onto."

Of the three of us, Jilly seemed the most without a rudder. Even Dylan had her band of thieves and runaways as a surrogate family. Jilly had no one to call her own, which made her seemingly sunny optimism all the more chilling because I had no idea how it could be real or where it could be coming from.

"We'll see," Dylan said, reaching for the tequila bottle and pouring herself a shot. Not to be a prude or anything but it seemed a little early to be hitting the bottle. However, I wasn't her mom so whatever, Dylan could drink herself stupid for all I cared. "So, what happens if your friend goes to the cops anyway?"

Dylan wasn't going to let it go. I finished my plate of spaghetti before answering with a short, "Then, I'll handle it" to put an end to the conversation. "How about this? You worry about your shit and I'll worry about mine."

"Yeah, except your shit is my shit and Jilly's too. Don't you think it's a bit fucking selfish to go off and do whatever the hell you feel like doing without thinking about how it might affect us?"

I liked to think of myself as the level-headed and fair one in this trio but damn, Dylan managed to point out how I was a fucking hypocrite.

"Fine," I said with a glower. "It was selfish of me to talk to Lora before talking to you guys first. Are you happy? Do you feel better?"

"Yeah, a little," Dylan answered with a tiny smirk. "Don't you feel better admitting that you acted like a little bitch who could've got all of us killed?"

I rolled my eyes. "A little dramatic don't you think?"

"Not really."

"Look, I conceded your point. That's all you're going to get from me so take the win and shut the fuck up about it, okay?"

Dylan smiled and downed another shot. "Fine," she said, capping the bottle. "I'll be gone tonight. Got a job with Badger. You good here?"

I gave her a mock salute. "All good, boss. No plans to sneak off."

"Good. Lock the door behind me."

"You're not my mom," I called after her, locking the door as she left. I let out a long sigh, tired as fuck. Emotionally I was spun out. I didn't know how long I could live like this. I wasn't ready for this to be my new reality but I didn't have any other options just yet.

At least my belly was full. Badger was a scary dick but he made a mean pot of spaghetti. The best my mom could do was box mac and cheese and never the actual brand kind but the generic shit that tasted like the cheese powder had been scraped off the cement walls of a cheese factory.

Jilly joined me at the table. "You know, she doesn't mean to be such a hard-ass about everything. She was really worried when you didn't answer your phone."

"I had it on silent and it was in my backpack," I said. "I would've answered if I'd seen it ringing. I guess I hadn't expected anyone to call." I paused a minute then added, "I'm sorry about worrying you guys. I wasn't thinking."

"I understand. Makes sense. I mean, I get why Dylan didn't think it was a good idea but I get why you had to do it, too."

I smiled, appreciative of her support. A part of me wanted to hold myself back from Dylan and Jilly. They weren't people I would've met and befriended organically but whether we liked it or not we were bonded together. I didn't know what that meant for the future but for now, we were stuck.

"So...did you tell your friend everything that'd happened?" Jilly asked, curious.

"The Cliff Notes," I answered. "I left out some of the more upsetting elements of the story."

"Everything was upsetting," Jilly said, adding, "Except the massage part. That felt really good. But then it was ruined by the enema situation. I had no idea enemas were so disgusting."

I laughed despite the topic. "Yeah, I can go the rest of my life never experiencing that again." For that matter, the waxing, too. I nodded, agreeing, "The massage was really nice."

The memory of what the masseuse whispered to me before I was shuffled on stuck to me. "I got the impression the masseuse was once an auction girl, too."

"Yeah? Why do you think that?"

"A hunch? She seemed to know a lot about The Avalon and how things were run but she whispered something to me privately and it felt like she was trying to help me."

"Like what?"

"She said, 'Be pleasant and agreeable. It's the only way.'"

"Meaning?"

I think she meant if I pleased my buyer I might get an offer to elevate and that would be the only way to walk out alive from this deal." I bit my lip as I recalled the memory. "And there was a sense of urgency to her tone even though she tried to hide it. The only way she would've known that I was in danger of never coming back was if she'd been through it before."

"So how does Madame Moirai get these girls to stay on and work for her?" Jilly asked. "I would think that they'd run as soon as they got the chance?"

"I don't know. Maybe they're just as much trapped as we were? I'm willing to bet my front teeth Olivia was an auction girl, too. She refused to admit it but I know she was."

"Well, there's no freaking way that thick-handed brute fo a woman who ripped all the hair from our bodies was ever an auction girl. The woman's body was a square and her face was scary enough to make babies cry."

"I don't think Madame Moirai fills her entire staff with auction girls but definitely people who have a reason to remain loyal."

I thought of Olivia, the one who'd shown us to our rooms, locked us in and then after we'd been brutalized and brought back broken, had shown little to no compassion for our pain. I really hoped she burned when I set that place on fire. I didn't care if she'd been an auction girl at one time, she'd sold what was left of her soul and she deserved a fiery death.

I looked to Jilly. "Is there really no one from your past that you miss?" I asked.

"No, not really. My foster parents were the worst sort and I never got close to foster siblings and because I switched schools a lot, I never made connections there either. I do miss school though. I liked to learn."

"What was your favorite subject?"

Jilly smiled. "Behavioral studies. Psychology. That kind of stuff. Anything that deals with the human mind. At my last school, I was hoping we'd get to dissect a cadaver brain but I guess that's not a thing until you get to college with more specialized courses. Not high school."

"That didn't gross you out?" I asked.

Jilly's blank smile was a little chilling. "No? Why should it? It's not like I knew the dead person, right?"

"You're a little macabre, you know that?"

Jilly laughed as if I'd just paid her a compliment, saying as she rose. "I know. Dibs on the shower."

And then she disappeared behind the warped bathroom door, humming.

Something definitely wasn't right with that girl. Hopefully, Madame Moirai hadn't completely broken what the foster care system had cracked.

I had to admit, even if I didn't want to, I was

starting to care for the quirky girl. Sometimes she was disturbing but there was also something endearing about Jilly that I couldn't quite shake.

I guess we were tied together for the foreseeable future and we had to make the best of it.

9

I felt like a caged animal. Days had gone by and Badger hadn't produced the private investigator he promised. Dylan was busy running jobs and Jilly seemed content to watch television or sleep all day.

I refused to let this become my new reality. I couldn't believe Dylan wasn't more careful about running jobs when anyone from The Avalon could catch her off-guard. It would take all of one minute for a van to pull up alongside Dylan, shove her inside, and disappear.

But when I reminded them of that fact, I was being "paranoid."

Both Dylan and Jilly seemed to have forgotten that we were sitting ducks if we didn't find some way to protect ourselves.

Cranky without an outlet, I prowled the small apartment vacillating between taking my chances back at home or just taking what cash we had left and bailing. It was all desperate thinking because I knew I wouldn't do either of those things but I couldn't take much more of this without movement. I needed to know we were doing something to bring down The Avalon. I needed Madame Moirai's head on a stick. I needed to know that Tana's death wouldn't go unanswered.

But the magnitude of this Herculean task was suffocating me. Hopelessness was a dangerous thing. It crushed everything good and light inside you until there was nothing but a leaden anchor in the pit of your stomach that made every step a challenge.

I didn't want to sit in this apartment. Not tonight.

Dylan was gone doing God knew what and Jilly was already dozing on the sofa, ready to call it a night.

I couldn't do it.

The muffled thump of raucous club music bumped beneath our feet, the nightlife coming alive as the DJ started the party. It was ten-thirty and I wanted to go out. I wanted something to help me forget the nightmare in my head that idle time kept playing on a loop without stopping.

I went into the bedroom and opened the closet. I had no idea who the clothes belonged to, Nova, maybe someone else Badger had staying here, but I found a top I liked and tight mini-skirt that fit and put them on. An old but decent pair of heels were in the back of the closet, too. I came out dressed and ready to go. Jilly woke up briefly to frown in confusion. "Where are you going? And why do you look like a hooker?"

"When in Rome, I guess," I returned with a flippant smile. "I'm going downstairs to check out the club. I'm taking some cash."

"Is that a good idea?"

"Seems to be okay for Dylan," I retorted, being pissy. Jilly frowned, pursing her lips as my comment was uncalled for but I didn't care. "If I stay in this apartment a minute longer Madame Moirai won't have to worry about killing me because I'll do it myself."

"That's drastic," she grumbled but she seemed to understand. After a long yawn, she said, "Fine. Whatever. Be careful. Don't let anyone roofie your drink."

Being roofied seemed like child's play after what we'd been through.

I tucked the cash into my bra and left.

Being as Badger owned the club, he had a private entrance, which enabled me to bypass the bouncer and the age check. Besides, if anyone gave me trouble, I'd just drop Badger's name and that ought to take care of any issues.

I was feeling reckless as fuck. It was dangerous to feel this way when there was nothing safe about my situation but sometimes danger made you feel alive and I needed an infusion of life right now.

The music throbbed in time with the lights strobing in the darkened gloom while bodies writhed with sexual abandon. The smell of bodies crammed together tickled my nose while the floor was sticky with spilled liquor or whatever else was thrown around in this place.

I went straight to the bar and ordered a double shot of whiskey. No one could roofie my drink if it went straight back in one gulp. I made short work of the shots and then made my way to the dance floor. I wanted to dance and lose myself at least for a night. I wanted to forget about everything and just feel good again.

In the darkness, surrounded by strangers, I

wasn't the girl who fucked everything up and ruined her life by making a stupid decision with a bunch of shady strangers. I wasn't the girl who hadn't known how she was going to pay for college but had been too afraid to tell her best friend. I wasn't the girl whose mother was a sloppy drunk held together by bad decisions and sheer force of will. I was just another faceless girl trying to lose herself in the moment and let the music heal whatever fracture hurt the most.

But inside everything was broken and the music wasn't enough. I pushed my way back to the bar and ordered more shots. If the benefit of living above the club didn't mean I couldn't get shit-faced drunk and then stumble home, I didn't know what the hell good it was.

No one would recognize me in this place. It was too dark and there were too many people. I was relatively safe. Except some frat guys, probably from NYU were jockeying to buy my next drink and even though I knew I should tell them to fuck off, I was almost out of the cash I'd stuffed in my bra and I wanted to keep drinking.

"Haven't seen you around, you new?" Frat Boy #1 said, looking me up and down with a leering grin. "You a freshman?"

"Technically, a senior," I answered, privately laughing at the lie. Well, not actually a lie, I was a senior in high school, but whatever, *details*. "Let me guess, NYU?"

"How'd you know?" Frat Boy #1 said, puffing his chest as if he'd accomplished something.

"Lucky guess."

"Where do you go to school?" Frat Boy #2 asked, trying to wedge himself into the conversation. "You look familiar."

"Do you watch a lot of porn?" I asked. Their shocked and vaguely uncomfortable expressions made the joke even better. I laughed, saying, "I'm kidding. I'm sure you don't know me." But I also bypassed the question, adding, "Who's going to buy me another drink?"

Both guys threw down money, gesturing to the bartender. I was already feeling it. My head was woozy and I felt light and airy. I confided in Frat Boy #1, leaning in to say, "I don't usually drink. My mother is a raging alcoholic. They say it's in the genes. I try not to do anything that will shake up that DNA but I've had a really shitty two weeks and at this point, becoming an alcoholic doesn't seem so bad. I mean, my mom doesn't seem to mind so maybe I'll give it a shot."

"I feel you," he said, trying to commiserate. "My dad threatened to cut off my allowance, like I'm supposed to get a job and go to school? Total bullshit. He's the one who pushed me to go to NYU in the first place so he can keep paying me to stay here."

Boo-freaking-hoo. I bit my tongue. Actually, this was exactly the kind of guy Lora would probably end up. Boring ass white guy with a stereotypical chip on his shoulder that smelled a lot like fucking entitlement. I didn't want him to buy my drinks anymore.

I smiled and said, "It's dancing time," and left him behind.

But he tried to follow. I was annoyed to find him in my space. Doing his jerky dance moves, trying to look sexy and I wanted to run away. I didn't want a dancing partner, just someone to keep buying me drinks but nothing ever came for free.

And I wasn't interested in paying for a few shots of cheap booze with my body for this dickhead.

I'd never sell my body again. To no one, for no amount of money.

Tears stung my eyes and turned away so he wouldn't see me cry but his hand on my waist made me stiffen in alarm. I whirled around and pushed him away. "Consent, jackass. Take a lesson," I growled like a feral animal. "Touch me again and I'll kick your nuts into your throat."

Frat Boy #1 held his hands up in surrender and backed away, leaving me alone. I smiled and let the music take control.

At some point, after a few more shots, I found myself slumped on the dirty floor on the way to the bathroom. I hadn't made it. I was in and out of awareness and I wanted to get back to the apartment but I couldn't quite remember how to do that.

I must've mumbled Badger's name to someone — maybe the bouncer or something — and suddenly he appeared, collecting me from the floor and helping me up and out of the club and back up the stairs to the apartment. I stumbled but he caught me. He smelled of burritos and sweat — a weird combination — but it wasn't disgusting like you might think. Kinda made me hungry. Maybe I should've eaten before drinking myself stupid.

He helped me to the sofa and gently laid me down. The room was spinning. I might throw up.

"You gonna puke?" he asked.

"Maybe."

He got a bucket and put it near me. "Don't puke on the floor."

"Such a gentleman," I slurred, pushing down the

rising bile in my throat. "Thanks for helping me upstairs. I couldn't remember how to get here." *Or how my legs worked.*

"What the fuck are you doing?" he asked. "That was real stupid."

"Yeah, well, I'm a kid. I'm supposed to do stupid shit, right?"

"You're not a kid. You're like us. Being a kid is a luxury we didn't get."

I didn't have a response. He was right. My childhood had been snatched a long time ago. Way before Madame Moirai had put those fake ass documents in my hand, promising a way out but never planning to deliver.

"Where's the fucking P.I. Badger? You promised to help."

"Your problems are not my biggest problem," he said.

"Fuck you," I said, my head lolling back. "What about Nova? I thought you wanted revenge for what happened to your sister?"

"Careful," he warned. "Just because you're drunk don't mean you can't get popped in the mouth for saying what you shouldn't."

"You'd hit a woman?"

"If she fucking earned it, sure."

"That's fucked up. You're a real dick."

He chuckled. "And you've got balls of steel for a tiny white girl."

"I'm a little Native American, too," I said.

"All right, Pocahontas. Go to sleep."

"Hey, that's racist and offensive," I said, my eyes drifting shut.

"Yeah, well, I'm a dick, remember?"

Can't argue with that.

Seconds later, I was blissfully unaware of anything.

And it was the best sleep of my life.

Maybe embracing my alcoholic roots wasn't such a bad idea after all.

10

I woke to Dylan scowling at me. I rose to a seated position, my head throbbing like an evil monkey was using my brain as a drum, to ask sourly, "What's your problem?"

"You. You are my problem," Dylan said emphatically.

"Fuck, it's too early and my head hurts too much to deal with whatever your drama of the moment is," I said, rising on wobbly feet, the room still spinning. I went to the sink and slurped water straight from the tap. Then, splashed the cold water on my face, hoping it would help the misery in my head. I groaned when it didn't.

Drying off, I was grateful to see a pot of coffee ready. I poured myself a cup and returned to the sofa, feeling like an old lady who'd been ridden hard by life and put away wet. Dylan was still staring a hole into my head. "What?" I asked, exasperated. "Fucking spit it out already."

"Have fun last night?" she asked.

"I guess. Why?"

"Because I heard Badger had to save your drunk ass."

Was this Dylan's brand of jealousy? Like I'd purposefully hoped Badger would run to my rescue? Good grief, she was off-base and I wasn't about to argue stupid shit. I shrugged. "I needed a change of scenery. Unlike you, who gets to run around like nothing happened, I'm stuck in this fucking place day in and day out. I'm going insane. And, fuck you, for daring to call me out when you've done nothing but run away from this situation since coming back. You're home, Dylan. We're not."

"I found us a place to crash so we're not staying in old churches and stealing from yuppie vacation homes," she said. "Now you're crying because you don't get to cuddle up in your own bed at night?"

"Give me a break, it's not like that and you know it. Don't pretend that you don't have the better end of this deal. I'm not saying I'm not grateful but what we're doing right now, doesn't end with anything but more of the same. We're not any safer here in this apartment than we were in the abandoned church. Madame Moirai is going to find us if we don't find her first. Badger promised he'd help. Well, where's the fucking help?"

Jilly appeared in the bedroom doorway, standing in her t-shirt and long socks. Obviously, she'd over-heard us because we weren't trying to be quiet. "It's not so bad here," she said. "It's a nice apartment. I mean, I've stayed in worse. At least there's running water and a working toilet."

Way to keep the bar low. "Wake up, Jilly, this isn't safe and even if it were...what happens next? You plan to spend the rest of your life watching cartoons and hiding from the world? Eventually, Badger is going to want his apartment back. This is a temporary fix for a fucked up situation that's not getting any less fucked up by ignoring it and hoping it will go away."

"Don't yell at me. I told you we had enough cash to get to California," Jilly muttered, folding her arms across her chest. "You're the one who wanted to come to the city. We're never going to do jack shit against Madame Moirai. She has endless resources and we don't have shit."

"I'm not giving up," I fired back. "If nothing else,

I'm going to make sure Henri Benoit gets what's coming to him."

"And how are you going to do that?" she asked, shaking her head. "It's not like you're going to bump into him at the country club. You don't even know where he lives."

"But I can find out, somehow," I said, refusing to give up. "That's what the P.I. is for." I returned to Dylan, "And why do you care if Badger saved me when I was a drunk mess? What does it matter?"

"Because you shouldn't get it into your head that Badger is a good guy because he's not."

"I wouldn't worry," I retorted, irritated that Dylan was being so damn irrational about something so stupid. "It's not like I'm going to fall head over heels in love with Badger because he dragged me up a flight of stairs and gave me a bucket to puke in."

"Good because that's the last thing I need to deal with," Dylan said.

"How about you worry about yourself and keeping a low profile and I'll worry about myself," I said. "The other day it felt like there were a million eyes on me. I wouldn't put it past The Avalon to have contacts with access to the traffic cams and shit. Being out in the open is dangerous for us."

"Who says I'm out in the open," Dylan scoffed as

if I were naive. It's true I didn't know how Dylan operated when she was running a job for Badger and frankly, I didn't want to know. Sometimes, I didn't want to know Dylan at all.

"Are you finished busting my balls over this? My head is on fire."

Dylan paused regarding me with a speculative stare as if gauging whether or not she believed me, then nodded, reaching into the end table drawer to pull out a bottle of aspirin and toss them at me. "Here," she said.

I had the wherewithal to catch the bottle, surprised at how lightning quick Dylan's moods could change.

One minute she was the devil and the next, a benevolent angel dispensing meds.

I gulped aspirin with a swallow of coffee and closed my eyes, waiting for the medication to work.

Jilly exhaled a long sigh. I opened my eyes when she joined me on the sofa. "I know we can't stay here forever," she admitted. "I just don't know what to do. Nothing feels safe. I'm afraid of my shadow right now. Every time I turn around I feel like someone is going to snatch me out of thin air and I'm going to end up on a slab somewhere like Tana."

I got it, I felt the same. "We have to do something,

if only to feel like we're not going down without a fight. If they're going to win no matter what, I want to be the biggest pain in their ass ever. I want them to wish they never offered us the deal."

"What do you think they do with all those bodies?" Dylan asked, frowning in thought. "I mean, think about it, assuming they only keep the ones they elevate...that means they've got to have a place to dump all those girls that don't make the cut."

"Like a mass grave?" Jilly asked, shivering. "That's a gross thought."

"Everything about their operation is gross," I muttered with a glower. "I hope that place burned to the ground. At least then Tana wouldn't be thrown in wherever the other girls ended up."

"Like Nova?"

Sad for Dylan, I nodded. "Yeah, possibly." Although there was still a chance Nova was alive. "You know, maybe Nova got elevated. We don't know that she's dead."

"I can't cling to a small hope that she's alive," Dylan said. "It's easier for me to deal with the pain if I think she's gone. Besides, I can't imagine the hell of being elevated with those sadistic assholes. Better to be dead."

I didn't disagree. If I'd been stupid or desperate

enough to take Henri's deal there was no telling what he would've done to me if he thought I'd belonged to him. I stuffed down a shudder, feeling the phantom slide of his fingers across my skin. I would never let that man touch me again. I'd rather die first.

Abruptly, I said, "I think he has kids." Both girls were confused. "My buyer," I clarified. "I think he has a family somewhere. How does a father and a husband do that to another human being?"

"Because they're two-faced narcissistic liars," Dylan answered bluntly. "They don't care about anyone or anything but themselves and they don't feel an ounce of guilt for what they do."

"Still, hard for me to understand."

"Don't try," Dylan said. "Better to bury that shit."

But I didn't want to bury it. I wanted to keep it front and center so I never forgot or forgave what'd been done to me. I wanted to watch them all burn but I didn't know how to make it happen. At the end of the day, I was still a kid without any money, resources or help. Miracles weren't exactly something I was used to getting so I never looked for or expected them.

"I need access to a computer. A simple Google

search might bring up Henri. I have to at least try," I said.

"You could go to the library, that way the IP doesn't route back to this place," Jilly suggested.

"That's a good idea," I said. "I can't sit around anymore. I have to do something or I might as well just put a fucking bullet in my head myself."

"Don't go alone," Dylan said with a rare burst of protectiveness. "Watch your exits and keep your head on a swivel. Jilly, you should go with her."

"I love libraries," Jilly said. "Been a long time since I've been able to find a good book."

"You're not there to read Wuthering Heights, you're there as a look-out," Dylan reminded her with a scowl.

"Obviously," Jilly retorted, rolling her eyes. "But I can multi-task. Also, I'm kinda impressed that you know the title of a book, a classic, even."

"Why? I know how to read," Dylan said.

"You just don't seem the type to curl up with a book, that's all."

"And you don't seem the type who would sell her cherry to a stranger but we all have secrets, right?"

Jilly stuck her tongue out at Dylan. "You're such a mean bitch sometimes."

"Keeps me alive," she said.

Listening to these two fight was as enjoyable as pounding a nail in my foot. Rising with a wince as my head threatened to pop. "I'm going to shower and then we can go," I said to Jilly. "Can you be ready when I am?"

"Of course."

"Good." To Dylan, I said, "Can you put some pressure on Badger about that P.I.? I'm not messing around. I need action or..."

"Yeah, yeah, you're going to kill yourself, Drama Queen. I got it."

I smiled sweetly, saying, "Or you" before leaving them all behind. Maybe a shower wouldn't wash away the stain on my soul but at least I'd smell better. I was a disgrace. I think I might've puked a little on myself.

Dylan could play games all she wanted but I sensed that she was territorial about Badger, though God only knew why. If she thought I was eyeing Badger for anything other than a means to an end, she was nuts. For that matter, I couldn't imagine ever trusting anyone enough to let them into my private circle for as long as I live.

Sometimes I felt the rage and fear bubbling in the pit of my stomach turning everything rancid inside me. Did that ever go away? Was I going to carry this fetid stench with me until I died? The inability to do anything to Madame Moirai ate at me. I wanted them all to pay.

Somehow.

Bearing this burden felt heavier than I could handle but what choice did I have? None. I owed it to all the dead girls crying in silence, lost and thrown away, to bring down this awful operation, even if it killed me to do so. That was the cost of surviving. The debt that was due.

I would gladly pay it if it meant Madame Moirai and The Avalon went down in flames.

But gotta start somewhere. I was tired of waiting. Tired of hoping Badger would come through somehow. I learned a long time ago, if you wanted to be saved, you had to save yourself.

This was no different.

Badger was right about one thing — I wasn't a kid…and I haven't been for a very long time.

11

The library was a bust. A search revealed no record of a Henri Benoit, which meant that wasn't his real name. I tried not to let my disappointment show but I hadn't realized how much I wanted my search to reveal something substantial until it came up a big, fat zero.

Jilly rubbed my shoulders as we rode the subway back to the apartment. "It was worth a shot," she said, trying to make me feel better. "At least you can say you tried."

"I thought for sure that was his real name but I guess it makes sense that he wouldn't just share that information with an auction girl. What kind of fucking game are these people playing?"

"A dangerous one," Jilly answered, leaning her head on my shoulder. "Something will come up."

Her attempt at softening the blow only made me want to cry harder. We had less than nothing now. I'd tricked myself into thinking that at least having my buyer's name would mean something, that it gave us a leg up, an advantage in a rigged game but I was wrong.

We had nothing.

Madame Moirai always won in every scenario.

"I also did a search for any mention of the fire and there's still nothing. How would they keep that quiet?" I asked. "I set the mansion on fire. There should've been some mention of it somewhere. I don't understand."

"Money talks. Maybe they greased the palm of the local first responders," Jilly answered. "Doesn't seem too far-fetched that they probably paid off anyone who might've asked questions. Plus, we don't know how bad the fire got."

"I know the guards bailed. We saw them drive past us like they were on fire, too. For all we know that house burned to the ground. There were enough chemicals in that place to burn for days. They would've had to have help to put it out."

Jilly didn't have an answer but we knew the score. Madame Moirai had made sure that no mention of the fire would be found anywhere. They knew how to cover their tracks.

We were silent for the rest of the ride. By the time we got back to the apartment, we were hungry and grumpy but Badger had a surprise waiting for us when we walked through the door. I didn't have time to share our depressing news when Badger started talking.

"It's about time," he said from the kitchen. An older man, possibly in the tail-end of his forties or early fifties sat, leaning forward, looking edgy and uncomfortable. I took a wild guess that this was the private investigator Badger knew. The man looked like he hadn't shaved in weeks much less showered. There was a general sense of unkempt personal hygiene that spoke of a hard life and bad choices. Hell, he looked like exactly the kind of man my mom would date. Badger gestured grandly, saying, "Adrian Hicks, meet Nicole and Jilly."

Since Dylan was already there, he must've already introduced them. Not that Dylan looked happy or excited to have an adult in the room with some kind of police experience.

The man named Hicks looked us up and down, as if trying to decide whether or not he'd take the job based on first impressions, which I thought was fucking rich. I beat him to the punch because I didn't like being judged, saying to Badger, "This is your private investigator? He looks like a fucking drunk."

"Beggars can't be choosers," Badger said with a scowl meant for me but then he looked to Hicks and said, "But I guess we could ask him...Hicks, you drunk?"

"Not enough for a gig like this," he growled, his voice ravaged by a lifetime of smoking and booze. To Badger, he added, "I want my fucking deposit upfront in case this turns out to be a huge waste of time."

Badger produced a wad of cash but before Hicks could grab it, he jerked it out of range. "I don't care if you end up drinking yourself stupid, just remember what happens when people I hire don't hold up their end of the bargain." He let Hicks take the cash with a smirk. "We understand each other?"

"Such a tough guy," Hicks drawled, tucking the wad into his worn jean pocket, then lit a cigarette as Badger left us alone. After a long speculative drag, he said, "So what's this I hear about conspiracies and shit?"

This guy didn't fill me with a lot of confidence but like Badger said, we didn't have the luxury of being choosy. "Have you ever heard of something called The Avalon?" When he lifted a shoulder with a blank stare, I shared, "Well, that's who we're up against. From what we can tell, The Avalon is the network that these assholes hide behind. They're all rich perverts."

"Ain't no crime to be rich," he said.

"It's not that they're rich. They're killing girls."

"How do you know?"

Exasperated, I said, "Didn't Badger tell you anything about this case?"

"I like to hear it straight from the horse's mouth. Gives me a chance to look someone in the eye while they're telling it."

"I'm not lying," I said, offended. "Why would I lie about this?"

He shrugged again. "People lie for all sorts of reasons in my experience."

I was getting hot under the collar. Jilly interjected before I could say something I might regret. "Are you a good private investigator?"

"I'm the best little girl," he said without an ounce of humility.

Dylan cut in, "Yeah, well, I guess we'll be the

judge of that," folding her arms across her chest. "And don't call her a little girl. We've seen and been through shit you couldn't imagine."

I nodded to Dylan, agreeing.

"Fair enough," he said with surprisingly somber appreciation. "Tell your story."

I shared a look with Jilly and then after drawing a deep breath, launched into our story from start to finish, leaving out nothing, even though my throat closed up a few times in the telling. I even added the small bit I knew about Nova but admittedly, my information was limited and Dylan didn't seem ready to add her two cents just yet.

He didn't show a flicker of emotion the entire time but I sensed the energy change between us. The laziness in his gaze narrowed to full-alert as he listened. I ended with my discovery that my buyer had given me a false name and that we now had nothing else to go on. "I hope you have some tricks up your sleeve," I said. "Because we've got no leads at this point."

Hicks grunted, stubbing out his cigarette. "That's one helluva story."

"Do you believe me?"

He didn't hesitate. "I do. Reminds me of a few

cases that cropped up when I was a detective. Never were able to solve. Filed under cold cases and never touched again."

I swallowed. "Is that what happens to dead girls when no one cares enough to keep looking for answers?"

"More times than not," he admitted. "Trust me, it never sits well with a detective when they can't close cases but there's always a few that slip through the cracks."

I thought of Tana. "We have to stop these bastards before they abduct a whole new crop of auction girls. They're never going to stop unless we make them."

"Hold up," he said, raising his hands to slow me down "it's not that easy. If it's a bunch of rich people being shielded by this shadow organization, it will be a bitch trying to figure out where the core is."

"But you can do it, right?" Jilly asked.

"Let me make some calls. I have a contact in the NYPD Detective Bureau. Let me see if I can't get her to make some inquiries."

"Be careful," I prompted, almost out of habit. I clarified, shifting on my feet. "I mean, the people we're dealing with are really dangerous and I wouldn't doubt that they have dirty cops on the payroll. The last thing I need is the one person able to help us getting whacked for talking to the wrong people."

"Don't worry about me. You worry about you. Stay low and wait until I contact you."

"What do you mean? I can't sit in this apartment like a caged canary. I'm already going crazy."

"Give me a day or two. I'll get back to you as quick as I can," he assured me.

That wasn't the answer I was hoping for but it was the most logical. Hicks let himself out and then it was just Jilly, me and Dylan.

"You think he can help us?" I asked the girls.

Dylan shrugged as she picked at her cuticle. "He seems like a crusty old drunk but, I don't know, he's got more contacts than we do, right?"

I nodded. "Yeah, I guess so." But nothing felt right and the odds were so stacked against us, I couldn't help but choke on the despair closing my throat.

"Why do you think he knows Badger?" Jilly asked, curious. "Seems weird for a guy like him to know an ex-cop."

"Badger collects people. He says you never know when you're going to need to call in a favor."

"Do you know Hicks?" I asked.

"No. Never met him before in my life but Badger doesn't share. He's a fucking locked box, you know? He keeps his secrets close to the vest and for good reason. Honestly, I don't want to know too much about Badger and how he operates. Better that way. Better for all of us."

I knew I shouldn't look a gift horse in the mouth but after the way I was raised, I learned to question everything. No one was purely innocent. And that included me. I never should've taken the deal but I had. A normal person would've run away from an offer as crude and dangerous as the one we were offered. I knew this because just sharing what'd happened to me with Lora had been completely horrified.

Had I been horrified when I was approached, when the pen was put to paper? Not really. Nervous, yes; horrified, no.

But I should've been. I should've run so fast that my shoes caught fire.

And what about Tana? How had she managed to scribble her name on the dotted line when she'd clearly been scared to go through with it?

I looked to Jilly and Dylan. "What were your

plans if Madame Moirai hadn't come along and dangled the promise of a new life in front of you?"

Jilly frowned, shrugging. "I dunno. I didn't really have a plan. I just liked to get from day-to-day. Maybe spend some time at the beach. Relax. Soak up the sunshine." Jilly seemed to hear herself. A turbulent ocean of awareness washed over her expression. "You know, planning for a future was never an option for me. You get used to drifting, to surviving and there's no room for long-term planning. You just want to exist somewhere."

"Did you think the money would change that?" I asked.

"Maybe."

"It wasn't like we were going to walk away with millions," I said. "That's not enough to live on forever."

She lifted her shoulders in a quick motion, a ready smile forming. "I'm pretty good at living in the moment. I guess I just would've done that."

I returned to Dylan. "And you?"

Dylan wasn't a sharer. I half-expected her to shut me down with a rude comment. She didn't but her dead-pan answer almost made me wish she had.

"What does it matter? We can't change what we did or what we didn't. I didn't take the deal for the money. I did it for Nova. In the end, I didn't get either."

Somehow glimpsing a sliver of Dylan's raw pain was like drinking bleach with a fatalistic smile because you knew the world was burning.

And that's all I could say about that because it kinda killed me.

12

The three of us had become accustomed to sleeping in the same space. Jilly always took the middle and had no problems cuddling up to one of us like a little kid. It used to irritate me but the comforting weight of her body against mine had become soothing.

I think it was the same for Dylan, though she'd never admit it.

There was nothing sexual about it. Actually, it was more like a sisterhood. Jilly was always more than happy to wiggle in between us. Dylan routinely complained about Jilly's cold feet and threatened to kick her to the floor. I rolled my eyes, knowing Dylan would do no such thing but I agreed with Dylan — Jilly's feet were like ice.

It was like the girl had zero circulation running through her veins.

But without realizing it, we'd adopted each other into a dysfunctional family of three, bound by the most fucked-up of forever-binding glue.

That'd become our new reality.

Until I awoke with a start, my heart pounding, a Klaxon alarm going off in my head.

My entire body tensed. Panic sweat drenched my skin as sensed something was wrong. Jilly stirred beside me but Dylan was also awake. I slowly met her gaze. We weren't alone in the apartment — and it wasn't Badger.

I nudged Jilly awake just as Dylan gently covered her mouth so she didn't scream.

Jilly's eyes flew open but she remained silent with a short nod of terrified understanding as Dylan removed her hand. I gestured to the living room. Dylan slid with the stealth of a cat from the bed and I followed. Jilly silently dropped to the floor and crawled under the bed. Dylan gestured for me to hide in the closet but I shook my head.

I wasn't going to cower in a closet while Dylan faced whatever was coming for us.

I snatched a baseball bat lying against the closet

door. Dylan pulled a knife hidden between the mattress and the box spring. There was a gun hidden in the kitchen but we had no way of reaching it in time.

Whoever was in our apartment, wasn't there to be neighborly. It was nearly three in the morning and they weren't looking to sell us Girl Scout cookies.

I held my breath and peered silently around the corner from the shadows.

Three figures, dressed in black, were in the apartment. First, they headed to the master bedroom, which was technically Badger's but he wasn't there. Finding it empty, they came our way, moving through the darkened apartment with a stealth that spoke of experience.

The Avalon had sent professional assassins to kill us? *Jesus, how would we survive?*

My fingers clenched the neck of the wooden bat, scared out of my mind, nearly pissing myself.

They were there to clip loose ends.

But I wasn't going down without a fight and neither was Dylan. I could almost feel Jilly shaking beneath the bed but she didn't have a weapon so what could she do?

We were sitting ducks. All we had going for us

was the element of surprise and a hard-core will to survive.

I could tell they were men by the way they moved. The first man crept into the room, a gun with a silencer in his hand. I swung like I was hitting for the World Series, the bat connecting with a jarring crack against his skull, spraying blood and whatever else against the bed and far wall. He went down and Dylan jumped on him with the knife, slicing his throat wide open.

I didn't have time to freak out over what we'd done; our element of surprise was gone.

Two more men flooded the bedroom. I tried swinging again but he deflected the blow and I stumbled, nearly going to the floor. The dark was our only ally. I heard Dylan screech as the other man lifted her off her feet and slammed her to the threadbare carpet. I kicked at my assailant, sweat slicking my forehead as pure adrenaline powered my limbs. My foot connected with a jawline, sending a riot of pain rattling up my leg but his angry grunt told me it'd been worth it.

"You little bitch," he growled, grabbing my leg and jerking me toward him. I spun like a crocodile, kicking and flailing. A gun went off and something hot seared the top of my shoulder. Holy fuck, was that a bullet? An acrid smell curled my nose hairs. He'd shot in my direction but missed my head. My grasping fingers found Dylan's knife that she must've dropped in the scuffle. I swung wildly. The knife sunk past muscle with a sickening squelch that made me gag. He grabbed wildly for me and I pushed the knife deeper, twisting as it sunk to the hilt, biting into his spine on the other side. He fell to the floor, landing with a hard thump as a death rattle gurgled from his throat. I tried to scramble to my feet but everything seemed to be happening in slow motion.

Dylan was on her back, her assailant had his hands around her throat. I could hear her choking and flailing but I couldn't get to her.

Suddenly, Jilly wiggled out from beneath the bed and launched herself at the man like a wild thing made of teeth and claws. He had no choice but to release Dylan so he could defend himself from Jilly. He yelled in agony as Jilly sunk her canines into his neck with a savagery that was both awe-inspiring and scary as fuck. I fumbled for the gun or the bat as Dylan gasped, trying to catch her breath. The man reached behind him and tossed Jilly as if she were made of straw. She crashed into the old dresser, giving him time to struggle to his feet, holding his neck where she'd chomped into him.

"The gun," Dylan cried out but the man already had it in his hand. Oh God, I was going to die. But just as the man pulled the trigger, two things happened at the same time blurring time and space right before my eyes.

Jilly had scrambled to her feet and tried to push the man's arm but ended up square in front of him as the gun went off, taking the full brunt of that shot as she crumpled forward. I screamed, trying to catch Jilly, uncomprehending as the man arched his back as if someone had pulled the hair from his head but in fact, it was the knife as Dylan had plunged it right into his liver.

He wasn't dead yet but he would be as he writhed in agony, the minutes of his life ticking by without prejudice. I didn't care, he deserved to die a horrid death. "Flip the lights," I screamed, still holding Jilly as she lay still in my arms. "Oh my God, Dylan...oh my God!"

Dylan, her face bloodied, mottled handprints bruising her neck, limped to the lamp and flicked it on, stumbling toward me. "Is she dead?" she asked, stricken and afraid.

"I don't know," I wailed, trying to keep pressure

on the wound in her stomach, watching in horror as it burbled past my fingertips like a broken pipe. "We need an ambulance!" But Dylan ignored my frantic cry and knelt beside Jilly, gently searching for a heartbeat. "What the fuck are you doing? Make the call!"

"She's already dead," Dylan said, choking on a sob. "She's gone." Rocking back on her heels, she covered her face as her shoulders shook with tears but I couldn't accept it. Couldn't accept that within a heartbeat, Jilly was gone.

Minutes ago we'd been in that bed, sharing a tight, cramped space, clinging to each other for warmth and security and now she was dead?

"No," I mourned, holding her limp body tightly to mine. "No, no no!" I refused to allow this to happen. I glared at Dylan through a sheen of tears. "Call. The. Fucking. Ambulance."

But Dylan snapped out of her shock and bounded to her feet, gesturing wildly to the dead people everywhere, her shrill voice strangled. "And how do we explain this? Huh? Got any bright ideas on how we explain that we just murdered three men? For all they know, we might've killed Jilly, too! No one is on our side on this. This is your fucking fault anyway. You just had to go talk to your friend, didn't you? Now, they know where we live!"

Dylan's hissed accusation cut into my soul.

I blinked back in stunned, horrified silence as Dylan stomped from the room, leaving me with four dead bodies, one of which was still cradled in my arms. Was this my fault? Had I caused Jilly's death? I held Jilly, tears flowing down my face. What the fuck just happened? I didn't know what to do. I couldn't let go of Jilly but I knew we couldn't stay. Grief and shock mingled in an entangled mess until I couldn't breathe around the horror building in my brain.

"It was self-defense," I whispered to Jilly even though she couldn't hear me. "They were going to kill us." I adjusted her dead weight in my arms, ignoring the ache in the protesting muscles. I wouldn't let her go. She saved my life. "Why'd you do that, Jilly?" I cried quietly. "Why did you jump in front of the gun?"

But Jilly couldn't answer. She'd never answer another question again. Never try to mediate between me and Dylan. Never insert her scary optimism into a conversation or be blindly supportive and loyal to whoever she believed was her friend.

Because Jilly didn't have real friends but she wanted to *be* a friend.

And she sacrificed herself for the people she cared about.

Me and Dylan.

A fucked up duo if there ever was one.

I ugly cried on that floor, holding Jilly's slowly cooling body until Dylan returned to drag me away.

We couldn't be caught in that apartment with four dead bodies.

We had to leave Jilly behind.

"C'mon, we gotta jet." Dylan had her backpack on, tossing mine to me. I was shaking from head to toe. "Badger will take care of this but this place is burnt."

"What's going to happen to Jilly?" I asked, my throat closing.

"The worst has already happened to her. She's dead. What happens from this point forward...Jilly isn't going to care."

Dylan was right but the horror of knowing that Jilly wouldn't have a dignified resting place was more than I could stomach. I ran to the toilet and barfed. I took a minute, resting my head against the cold rim of the toilet bowl, then rising on shaky legs, rinsed my mouth, changed my clothes and grabbed my pack to join Dylan.

My soul felt punched bloody but Dylan's blunt

realism spoke to my own pragmatism. We couldn't stay here anymore. If The Avalon sent three goons to kill us, once they realized that mission had failed, they'd send more until they finally succeeded.

I shouldered my pack and asked with zero emotion, "Where to now?"

"Until Badger can get us a new place, we'll go back to the church."

"What if they just follow us there, too?"

"They won't tonight. After that, we'll think of something."

I nodded. I didn't have much of a choice. We had to leave the scene of the crime. What had once been a safe place was now a hot-spot and we had to run.

First Tana, now Jilly, were we running away from the inevitable? Were our death warrants signed, sealed and delivered to the Grim Reaper? Maybe all of this running was pointless.

I didn't know how The Avalon had found us but they had.

If Dylan was right and they found us because of me, I'd never forgive myself. The shock had turned my insides numb.

I took one last look before leaving the apartment.

I'm so sorry, Jilly. You deserved so much better than anyone had ever given you...even me.

"Let's go," Dylan urged and I followed her out of the apartment. We ran into the night, careful to keep to the shadows and away from any obvious CCTV cameras.

Running was all we knew to do.

Nowhere felt safe.

13

We made it to the church, slipped inside and barricaded the door, just like before. Dylan made a quick call to Badger and returned to drop heavily onto the lumpy sofa, the frozen look of devastation mirroring my own.

"I don't know how they found us," I whispered against the scrape of guilt on my heart. "I swear I was careful."

"Well, they found us," Dylan said flatly.

Yeah, they found us. "And we killed them." I looked at my hands, remembering the feel of the knife as it'd ended the man's life — a man who had come to kill me and my friends. "They'll send more," I said. "What are we going to do?"

"I don't know."

"We should tell Hicks," I said.

"Chill out, let me think," Dylan snapped, pulling her knees up to her chest. The church was like a freezer but we didn't feel the cold. Nothing could compare to the desolate chill lodged in our souls. We were murderers now. Sure, it'd been self-defense but I knew nothing would ever erase the memory of the kill. I felt bile rise in my throat but I swallowed it down. I started to shiver. Dylan cast me an irritated look but reached over and pulled me close against her shoulder. Tears slid down my cheek to splash on my chest. Jilly was dead. The knowledge kept echoing in my head until I couldn't hear anything else. Dylan must've been suffering the same stone-cold reality because she said in a halting voice, "Jilly saved us. The silly shit saved us both. She could've run and gotten away but she didn't. Why didn't she run?"

"Because we were her family. A fucked-up, dysfunctional family but a family just the same," I said, wiping my nose on my sleeve. "And she'd do anything for family."

"Fuck," Dylan muttered, shaking her head. "Sons of bitches. I hope they suffered before they died."

"Me too," I said, giving in to my savagery. They

deserved to die. They'd come to kill three kids. They were as soulless as Madame Moirai. "I'd give anything to be the one to end that cunt. I want to watch the life bleed out of her."

Dylan knew exactly who I was referring to. She nodded. "Same."

"So what now?" I asked.

"I guess, sleep?"

"I can't sleep," I said, shaking my head. "I feel like I need to puke and shit myself at the same time."

Dylan motioned. "There's an empty bucket over there."

I eyed the bucket. How was this my life? In all the times I'd hated being with Carla, hating our abject poverty, at least I'd never had to shit in a bucket while trying not to puke my guts out at the same time. I guess it was true that you never really appreciated what you had until it was gone.

Even if all you had was a shithole with indoor plumbing.

I settled against Dylan, pulling the ratty blanket over us that smelled faintly of piss and ruin, just thankful for the warmth. "Do you believe in heaven?" I asked.

"No."

I glanced up at Dylan. "No? Not at all?"

"I don't know," Dylan admitted with a tiny shrug. "Maybe at one time I did. Now? I don't know." She paused, asking, "Do you?"

I didn't know either but I liked the idea of heaven. "Sounds like it could be cool if it were real. I like to think that if heaven is real, Tana is okay." My voice cracked. "And Jilly, too."

Dylan's hand found mine beneath the blanket, squeezing tight. "Yeah, me too."

I let my eyes close, the rush of adrenalin finally receding, leaving exhaustion in its wake. I didn't want to dream or think. I wanted the dark hole of oblivion to suck me up and bury me. If I didn't wake up, a part of me would be relieved. To die on my own terms seemed so much better than to die because Madame Moirai had ordered it.

I thought of Jilly. I was still in shock. I would miss her cold feet and sunny optimism. I would miss her ability to turn a situation into something less or more than it was depending on what was required. I would miss her constant surprising me with details about herself or her life before Madame Moirai and how I wasn't sure if she wasn't a cracked egg after all.

I would miss everything that Jilly was and would never be.

Like Tana.

Maybe it was fitting that it was just me and Dylan now. We were both assholes, both bitches on our best days, and now we had to find a way to destroy a network bigger than we were, with little to no resources.

On paper, it seemed like certain suicide.

How could we hope to prevail when no one was on our side? When no one cared? Who gave two shits about the girls lost to the machine?

Damn it, I cared.

I would make people care if it killed me.

And let's face it, it probably would kill me but it would be worth it.

Jilly never actually shared what'd happened with her and her buyer but it was likely the same as what'd happened with mine and Dylan's — sanctioned abuse.

What broke inside a person that made them believe it was acceptable to abuse another human being like they weren't a person the same as them?

As fucked up as my life was, I would never hurt someone the way Henri had hurt me, the way Madame Moirai had manipulated me into thinking I was doing something to make my life better when in fact, it'd made everything nightmarishly worse.

If I was willing to entertain the idea of heaven,

that meant I got to envision hell. While heaven was a nice thought, the idea of hell — and The Avalon roasting in it — made me happy.

Gleefully, actually.

I wasn't lying when I said I wanted to see them burn. I wish I'd been able to stick around and watch the auction house go up in flames instead of running for my life.

I would've roasted marshmallows and watched until every ember died into ash.

But like everything associated with The Avalon, my choices had been taken from me. Running and surviving had been my only options.

Just like now.

Tears stung my eyes even as I tried to hold them back. Dylan's light snore told me she'd dropped off already.

Dylan was hard as nails whereas I still had soft spots that bled when poked.

Deep down, I knew Dylan was devastated at losing Jilly but she couldn't possibly show that vulnerable of an emotion, not even to me.

Maybe with Nova but Nova was gone, too.

The Avalon had steamrolled our lives in unforgivable ways. Even though I wanted nothing more than to bury the memories so deep it would take an excavator to dig them out, I knew I had to crystallize every memory of the auction, Madame Moirai and my buyer. Any detail might lead to something useful. I would gladly suffer the flashbacks, the PTSD and the degradation if it meant that some detail I had locked in my head ultimately brought them down.

Right now, it felt like a pipe dream but shoot for the stars, right?

At some point, I fell into an uneasy sleep. Every sound jarred me awake. I shivered and shifted my stiff bones. Dylan moaned in her sleep but otherwise didn't stir. It was nearing morning. Dim, milky light pierced the dirty windows. I knew I wouldn't get any more sleep despite needing it. My eyes were filled with grit and my head hurt but my mind was already spinning.

Carefully removing myself from the sofa so I didn't jar Dylan, I grimaced as my bladder protested and eyed the bucket. Not much of a choice. I shimmied my jeans down and squatted over the bucket, relieving myself with a grateful sigh. With nothing to wipe with, I drip-dried and then pulled my pants back up. I would have to find a place to dump the bucket later. From what I remembered Jilly saying, this room had been the priest's office at one point. Why a priest had a sofa in his office I could only imagine but I suspected if that sofa could talk it might have some horrifying stories to tell.

Priests were just people and people were generally awful so, *there you go.*

But Jilly had once made this place her stomping ground. For whatever reason, this hole had made her feel safe when nothing else in the world had felt like a sanctuary.

I went to the old and battered desk and tested the stability of the ancient chair before fully seating myself. I slowly opened drawers, curious as to what might've been left behind. Not much. A few pens and pencils rolled forward, as if to say, "Here I am! Don't leave me behind!" but nothing else of value.

I leaned forward and rested my head on my folded arms. At this eye level, I saw something scratched into the soft wood top. I moved a little closer to get a better look. In the tiniest scrawl, I saw something that pricked the tears from my eyes.

Jilly Jewell Perez was here.

I traced the pad of my fingers over the carved cry for remembrance and squeezed my eyes shut. *Jilly Jewell.* How perfect was her name? She'd been a rare gem and I'd never forget her.

That's the crux of it, isn't it? We all wanted to be remembered. We wanted a legacy. We didn't want to fade into nothingness like a dream forgotten in the morning light. We wanted to matter.

But those without money didn't matter.

The lives of the auction girls didn't matter. We didn't come from rich families. They trolled the poor, disadvantaged and disenfranchised who were desperate for a sliver of hope, for something to cling to that didn't hurt or leave scars.

Henri (or whatever the fuck his name was) had pretty much said as much when he wouldn't allow me to ask if he'd offer up his kids to the auction. Let his friends pony up cash to fuck his daughters. He got pretty frosty at the idea.

Because *they* were better. *Their* lives mattered.

Mine didn't.

My blood had lesser value as it spilled. My skin was simply for his pleasure. As was my pain. I closed my eyes, riding out the wave of revulsion that always followed memories of Henri. He was the worst sort of monster — his supposed kindness was a game with rules he alone understood.

I won't cry. Not for him. Not for what he did to me. Not for what I lost. But I'll cry for Tana and Jilly...and even Nova, even though we'd never met. I'll cry for every single duped girl who'd been hoping for a fresh start by sacrificing some vital part of herself.

I'll cry for every girl who never had a chance to realize that she was worth so much more than the sum of her parts.

I'll cry for every girl lying in a cold, unmarked grave, mourned by no one and forgotten by everyone.

But I won't cry for him.

Not ever.

He could die with the rest of The Avalon assholes who thought because they had money, no consequence applied.

I would teach them that everyone had to pay at some point.

And their bill was way the fuck overdue.

I just needed a little help to figure out how to do it.

14

"Badger says to go to Hicks' place," Dylan said after receiving a message on her burner. We'd had no choice but to lay low in the church, waiting for instructions. We were too apprehensive about venturing out in broad daylight, which meant hiding in the church like two mice trying to outwit the cat. She shouldered her pack and waited for me to do the same. "Wear your hoodie, try to cover your face as much as possible."

I nodded, afraid to ask, "What about...the bodies we left behind?"

"He took care of it," she answered in a wooden tone. "C'mon, we need to get out of here."

We went out the back, avoided the CCTV street cameras and climbed the fire escape of Hicks' place and into the open window where the grizzled PI was waiting for us.

He quickly shut the window behind us and pulled the blinds down. I breathed a sigh of relief, happy to be somewhere that wasn't cold as a meat locker and sat heavily in the first chair near me, rubbing some warmth into my hands.

Hicks started talking first. "What the fuck happened?"

"Somehow they found us," I answered, hating that I was probably the weak link. "They got Jilly."

"Ahh shit," he muttered, shoving his hand through his wiry black and white peppered hair. "She seemed like a sweet kid."

"She was." I looked to Dylan, my throat closing. I couldn't continue. She'd need to tell the rest. Dylan understood.

"It was about three in the morning. Nicole and I woke up at the same time. We heard noises in the apartment that didn't feel natural. They sent three assassins to snuff us out but we took them out instead. Except, Jilly didn't make it out. She died saving us both."

Tears threatened to fall but I sniffed them back. I nodded, confirming Dylan's account. "She took a bullet to the gut," I said.

"Fuck, that's a shit way to die," Hicks said.

I glared. "Thanks. I think I already know that. I held her in my arms as she died."

"Sorry, kid," Hicks said. After a beat, he went to his kitchen and pulled a bottle of Jack, gesturing in offer, "You need some of this?"

I shook my head but Dylan accepted. They both downed a shot and then Hicks returned to sit opposite us, the bottle in hand. "You're in some deep shit."

"You think?" I returned caustically. I didn't have the mental bandwidth to entertain bullshit comments. "I need to know how they found us."

"You been staying out of sight?"

"As much as possible. I met up with a friend the other day but I stayed out of the CCTV line of sight and I wore a hoodie," I said. "I don't know how they found us."

"Retrace your steps," he instructed as he pulled a city map free from a cubby in his cluttered bookshelf, his gravelly voice rough with phlegm. Hicks wasn't a healthy man but his deep-set eyes remained sharp like a shark's. He unrolled the map, saying, "Don't leave out a single step."

I nodded and shared my exact route to and from The Cruller, ending with my subway ride back to the apartment as he traced with his finger my steps.

Hicks leaned back, nodding, then stabbed the map with his thick, calloused finger. "Right here," he said.

Both Dylan and I stared in confusion. "The subway?" I asked. "There aren't any cameras down there."

"Not that you can see. Hidden cameras were installed last year after the MTA got a big-ass grant to cut down on crime down below street level. You know those big silver columns? Well, it's got a closed-circuit camera system watching your every move, from every angle. So whatever they didn't catch up top, they caught down below. There's your mistake."

I blinked back tears. So it was my fault that Jilly was dead. I covered my face and leaned into my hands, afraid I was about to lose it. But Dylan didn't let me take all the blame.

"I didn't know about the cameras either," she said. "I've been using the subway for runs. Fuck, it could've been either of us that tipped The Avalon off."

I wiped at my face, so grateful for Dylan's grim admission. I couldn't survive the guilt thinking it'd been entirely my fault. As it was, I was teetering on the edge of a total melt-down. "So that means they have access to the feeds," I said, my voice strangled.

"That's my first guess," Hicks agreed, his brow wrinkling as he lit up a cigarette. "To be honest, I wasn't sure if you weren't just being a bit dramatic when I first heard your story but four dead bodies suggests that you weren't lying."

"Why would we lie about something like this?" I asked, incredulous. "What the fuck? You think we're on the run for funsies? We just lost someone we cared about. This is as real as a fucking heart attack."

Hicks wasn't ruffled by my venom. He rubbed at the scruff on his chin, thinking.

"What are we going to do?" I asked.

The silence grew tense as we waited. My heart-beat painfully against my chest.

Finally, after a long drag, he narrowed his gaze and said with a heavy sigh, "Here's the thing...I don't know if there's anything you can do."

"That's some shit advice," Dylan said. "Give up? Let them put us in the ground? What the fuck kind of advice is that?"

"I didn't say that," Hicks said, swigging straight from the bottle. "I said, fighting whoever the fuck these people are might be a lost cause and lost causes are bad for business."

"Badger already paid you, old man," Dylan

reminded Hicks with a growl. "There's no backing out now."

Hicks reached down into the nightstand cubby and pulled a book, revealing a hollow core, tossing the roll of cash back to Dylan saying, "And here's his money back. I don't take cases that have a zero chance of being solved."

Dylan tossed the wad back and he caught it with one hand. "And so is disappointing Badger."

Hicks finished off his cigarette and stubbed it out. "Kid, I sympathize with you but the thing is, I'm not going to blow smoke up your ass and tell you that everything is going to be okay when it's likely going to get you killed. My best advice, get off the grid, get out of the city, hell, get out of the state if you can, and try to start a new life elsewhere because this whole town is burnt for you by the looks of things."

That was his advice? That's what Jilly had wanted to do but Dylan and I had both known that if The Avalon could find us here, they could find us anywhere. I protested hotly, "There's no place safe enough from them. We're too big of a risk to leave running around. They'll come for us no matter where we run."

He didn't argue the point, just said, "Yeah, sorry kid. It's a shit hand."

"Fuck you," Dylan said, shaking her head in disgust. "Pretty easy to wipe your hands free of us, right? Must be nice to have shit for a conscience."

"Look, I feel bad for you. Is that what you want to hear? Fuck, it's a terrible situation, either way, you look at it but I don't have endless resources either. To fight this fight, you need bigger artillery than what I got. I'm trying to be honest with you."

Dylan's nostrils flared as she held back whatever was coursing through her veins — rage, fear, helplessness, take your pick — and muttered, "I need some fucking air," before slamming out the front door.

Dylan didn't like anyone see her crumple but I sensed she was struggling. She may be a bad-ass but she was still like me, overwhelmed and looking for someone to help before we all ended up dead and The Avalon continued, business as usual.

I didn't hold back the tears this time. I met Hicks' gaze even as he tried to avoid my stare. He shifted with discomfort, shaking his head, saying, "Your pitiful look isn't going to work. I've walked away from cases better than yours and I'm fucking immune to emotional manipulation." He shrugged again, "Like I said, I'm real sorry but there's nothing I can do."

My gaze snagged on a beat-up picture frame

lodged on the bookshelf, nearly hidden, of a little girl and what looked like Hicks during better days. He didn't look like a drunk beat-up by life in the picture. He looked healthy, happy and competent.

A far cry from the man drowning himself to avoid feeling anything.

I took a wild guess, gesturing to the picture, "That your daughter?"

He lifted his gaze to mine, narrowing his stare as if he'd rather not answer but he did. "Yeah. Cheyenne."

"Pretty name."

"Thanks," he grunted, still uncomfortable. "I can give you some train money to get you out of the city, maybe even out of the state but that's about the best I can do."

I ignored his offer. "How old is she?"

He rubbed at his forehead. "Uh, twelve. About to thirteen."

"I remember thirteen. Puberty. Good times."

"Yeah, well, she's with her mother so I'm sure that's all handled."

I started to put together a picture. There was no way Hicks brought his kid to this shithole. Not seeing how he used to live, how he used to be with his kid. This man was living in purgatory for sins he thought he owed penance. She looked about six in that picture, which meant, he probably hadn't seen his kid in six years if she was twelve almost thirteen now. Long time to be without your kid. My gaze fell on the bottle he was clutching like it was the only thing in his life that made sense.

I knew that look. I'd seen it plenty of times with Carla. He was an alcoholic.

"Why'd you lose custody?" I asked. He shook his head as if he weren't going to answer. I'd struck a nerve. *Time to keep pressing.* "You seem pretty close in that picture. She's cute. You miss her?"

"Every damn day," he admitted gruffly. "But she's better off with her mom."

"Maybe," I said, adding with a shrug, "probably."

He scowled. "No one fucking asked you, did they?"

"Well, you're a fucking mess and this place is a shithole. I wouldn't let my kid stay here either. I'm curious though...did your wife leave you because you're an alcoholic? Or did you do something really bad when you were drunk? I know some people like to pretend that alcohol made them do shitty things but I think it's just because deep down, they're shitty people and the alcohol made it easier for them to be their true selves." I paused a minute before asking,

"Did you molest your kid while you were drunk or something?"

I felt the violence in the air but as quick as it surged, it receded. Instead, Hicks shook his head, as if realizing what I was doing. "I never hurt my girl like that and never would. I lost my job and...lost everything else along with it."

Men were so ego-driven. Their self-worth was tightly tied to their ability to bring home the bacon. In Hicks' case, he let the pig get away. No more bacon. "That sucks," I said, trying to sound sympathetic. "But I'm sure your kid misses you."

He didn't believe me. "She's better off without me."

"Who knows? I guess you never will because you gave up."

"Enough with the motivational speeches, kid. Better and brighter than you have tried. Some things just aren't meant to be fixed."

I shrugged. "Yeah, probably right, but if you had a chance to take down the biggest, most disgusting human trafficking network in New York, I would think that you'd want to try if only for the simple fact that you don't want Cheyenne to end up like the rest of the auction girls."

His eyes flashed. "Cheyenne would never—"

"How would you know what your daughter would do? You haven't seen her in six years. Abandonment issues create daddy issues for girls. I'm sure you've seen plenty of what happens to girls constantly seeking approval from a dad that was never around."

There it is — the button I'd been searching for. I added, leaning forward and pinning him with a look to make my point, "Tana was a good girl and Madame Moirai still managed to get her hooks into her. What makes you think Cheyenne is safe?" I paused a beat, hardening my tone. "*No one* is safe from The Avalon unless you're in the Million Dollar Club and something tells me...you're not a fucking member." I rose and went to the door, ending with, "Call us when you find your balls."

And then I left to find Dylan.

15

A few days later Badger gave us a heads up that Hicks was coming to talk to us and to lay low until he showed up. We didn't have a choice but to settle in and wait in the church until Hicks showed up.

Silence was a mind-killer.

Dylan paced like a caged tiger and I chewed on my fingernails, replaying every bad decision of my life that lead up to me sitting in an abandoned church with no hope of ever having a normal life again.

I missed homework and overbearing teachers.

I missed the stale smell of booze and cigarettes that clung to the air in my apartment.

I missed the familiarity of routine that before, I couldn't wait to escape.

I risked a glance at Dylan. The quiet agony, the stuff she'd never share, brimmed in her eyes and I simply acknowledged it all with a nod because words weren't needed.

As bad as life had been, it was nothing compared to now.

By the time Hicks arrived, we were both a little feral and almost hoping it was The Avalon coming to end our misery.

But to our shock, Hicks wasn't alone and he made quick work of an introduction, gesturing to the middle-aged woman briefly, saying, "Dylan, Nicole, this is Kerri Pope, she's a detective with NYPD. You can trust her."

The woman, dirty blond hair tucked back in a low ponytail, had sharp eyes like Hicks but where he was hard and salty around the edges, she had a competent yet warm presence that I found genuine. Kerri nodded in greeting as I closed and barricaded the door out of habit. "Bad neighbors," I said by way of a small joke. To her credit, Kerri gave me a tiny smile before taking a seat on the lumpy sofa that served as our bed. Dylan hopped on the desk, eyeing both adults with wary suspicion.

"So you changed your mind about helping us, huh?" Dylan asked.

"Yeah, guess so," Hicks said, casting a quick look my way but didn't elaborate, going straight to business. "Kerri and I used to work together. I know she's trustworthy and she's a good person to have on your side. We're going to need someone on the inside if we're going to get anywhere. I've told her what I know so far but it's better if it comes from you."

Dylan looked bored but I knew this was her way of protecting herself. She couldn't take another rejection and neither could I but we had to start trusting someone if we hoped to survive what was coming for us. I took the plunge and shared our story. I didn't leave out anything, not even when my throat threatened to choke off my airway.

I could tell Kerri was struggling with the information and I couldn't blame her. If she was a good cop, learning that two kids just killed three assassins wasn't an easy pill to swallow. She'd have to fight her instincts and I knew all about that so I could sympathize.

"And you have no idea who these people are running The Avalon?" she asked.

"Nope," I answered with a resolute shake of my head. "If I did, I wouldn't be sitting here, I'd be wherever they were hiding so I could end their sorry lives."

Maybe I shouldn't talk so casually about murder seeing as I'd just confessed to killing someone but I figured the only way to find out if I could trust her was to put all my cards on the table.

Kerri nodded, digesting the information. "And where are the bodies now?" she asked.

"No clue," Dylan answered as if she didn't care because she probably didn't. Well, except about Jilly but Kerri hadn't been specific. "They were sent to kill us. If it hadn't been for me and Nicole's spidey-sense, we'd be dead right now. They were trained professionals with silencers on their guns. What else were we supposed to do?"

"If it was self-defense, you're protected by law," Kerri reminded us. "Are you sure you don't want to try and come down to the station and give a statement?"

Dylan scoffed. "Fuck no. The Avalon is clearly attached to someone with access to the CCTV feeds. I don't trust no cops to stick to their oath when a shit ton of money is waved beneath their nose."

"Not all cops are crooked," Kerri tried to say but Dylan wasn't interested and Kerri dropped that argument, switching gears. "All right, so let's talk logistics right now. You can't live in this church. You need a safe place to stay."

"Seems pretty safe to me," Dylan said, glancing around as if assessing our living space and finding it adequate even though it was abysmal and we were freezing our asses off at night. "No cameras and no one sneaking in to put a bullet in our brainpan while we sleep."

"You also could freeze to death," Kerri said, determining with a solid shake of her head. "It's too cold to stay here."

"We don't have anywhere else to go," I said. "It's not like we can just waltz into a hotel and get a room. Our options are pretty limited."

Kerri looked to Hicks, volunteering his place before he could stop her. "You can stay with Adrian. He's got a spare bedroom and no one would think to look for you there."

"Hold up," Hicks protested in alarm. "My place ain't good for kids. I'm not running a fucking daycare, Kerri."

"And they're not staying here. They're not toddlers. It's not like you need to child-proof your apartment. I'm not leaving them in this meat locker of a room to freeze to death. It's supposed to snow tonight. Temperatures will drop and without external heat, they will die here. If you want my help, you're going to have to pitch in, too."

Her blunt assessment was more than I expected but when Hicks folded with a sour look I was stunned. "Fine, but don't expect me to be some kind of gracious host or something. I'm not used to company."

"No one would ever accuse you of being a gracious host," Kerri returned dryly. "But it's the right thing to do and you brought me in for a reason so try to remember that." Something flickered between Kerri and Hicks, a remnant of feeling or emotion that maybe had to be kept under wraps, but was quickly squelched as Kerri moved on with the efficiency of a woman used to being in charge. "I'll start discretely searching through our missing person database and look for cases that may fit the criteria for this Avalon network. In the meantime, stay out of sight, stay out of trouble and try to keep a very low profile."

"That's pretty much what we've been doing *without* a babysitter," Dylan said pointedly.

Kerri didn't take the bait. "Good. Then it should feel familiar."

At least it would be warmer at Hicks' apartment and I wouldn't have to worry about rats or bugs crawling over me while I slept. Also, a toilet would be nice.

"Wait until dark before you make your move. Avoid all cameras, shield your face as much as possible," Kerri instructed, reaching into her pocket to pull out some cash and handing it to me. "And get something to eat. You're both very thin."

I shared a look with Dylan. We'd been keeping a tight rein on the stolen money we'd taken from the vacation house and whatever food we were eating came from the sporadic cooking habits of a man who seemed to think of food as an afterthought.

We'd both lost weight since fleeing the auction house but I hadn't had time to notice how my jeans were hanging from my bones. I curled my fingers around the cash, reluctant but grateful. I wouldn't admit it aloud but I was happy to let an actual adult start calling the shots, even if only for a minute.

Dylan, not so much, but she wasn't in a position to refuse.

I wondered how Badger would feel about his best runner being suddenly pulled out of commission. For that matter, I wondered how he handled the clean up on his apartment without tipping off law enforcement that something terrible had happened in that place.

I guess it wasn't my problem but it weighed on my shoulders as if it were.

Kerri stood, taking one final glance around our makeshift sanctuary, distress in her gaze but also understanding. As an NYPD detective, I'm sure she'd seen some shit. I was happy someone in authority actually seemed to care. She looked to me and Dylan, saying, "I'm sorry about your friend," and I could tell she meant it. Tears threatened to spill. I looked away with a sniff but couldn't get the words out. Kerri didn't press. Instead, she gestured for Hicks to follow and they left us behind.

Dylan returned the barricade after they were gone, then leaned heavily on the door. "You trust her?" she asked.

"I do," I answered.

"Why?"

"I don't know. There's something about her that feels real." I paused a beat. "Why? Do you get a different vibe?"

Dylan admitted with a shrug, "No, not really." She pushed away from the door to curl up beside me. "But I don't like the idea of shacking up with Hicks. What if he's a weirdo, sex perv or something?"

"He's not," I said, feeling pretty confident on that score. "He's an alcoholic who lost everything to his disease."

"What'd you say to make him change his mind?"

I shrugged. "I guess I just reminded him that second chances at redemption don't come often."

"And that worked?"

I barked a short mirthless laugh. "It would seem so. Time will tell, right?"

"Yeah, guess so."

Dylan looked to me, asking for the first time, "When you went to see your friend...what did she say when you told her what happened?"

I stared at my curled fingers. "She didn't know what to think. I'm not sure she believed me. Lora...her life isn't like ours. She has great parents and a bright future. I'm not even sure how we managed to stay friends this long because we have nothing in common."

"Maybe that's why," Dylan said. "Opposites attract and all that shit, you know?"

I nodded. "Maybe."

"But you wanted her to believe you."

"Yeah. I really did."

Dylan sighed. "Some people can't handle anything that challenges the way they see the world. It's not their fault, it's just the way they're hard-wired. For what it's worth, I'm sorry she let you down."

Yeah, me too. "Is Badger going to be okay with

you disappearing for a few days?" I asked. "He seems territorial."

"He's a fucking lunatic but he doesn't want the heat either. He knows I've gotta lay low for now. Besides, he knows where to find me."

"So what does Badger have on Hicks?" I wondered.

Dylan shrugged. "Who knows. Badger never gives up his leverage or his secrets. Right now, we can't afford to lose allies so whatever Badger's got on Hicks, is fine by me."

I agreed, leaning my head against hers. "Do you think we're ever going to be free of The Avalon?" I asked.

"I don't know. Seems pretty fucking bleak, if you ask me but I'm not the most optimistic person by nature. I want to believe that we've got a shot but, right now, feels kinda like we're treading water and a tsunami is right behind us."

Pretty accurate analogy.

Everything we were doing, maybe, in the end, none of it mattered because we were tiny specks in an ocean with waves big enough to send us straight to the sandy bottom with the rest of the dead auction girls.

I shivered, not only because it was cold but because fear had a chill all its own.

All I knew was that I didn't want to die.

All we'd wanted was a chance to live.

Why was that so wrong?

16

Living with Hicks was nearly as excruciating as living with Badger because men, at any age, didn't seem to notice or care about things like dirty dishes, overflowing trash and hitting the toilet with their stream of morning piss so it didn't splash all over the place like an out-of-control fire hose.

But beggars couldn't be choosers, which was probably something I was going to get tattooed on my fucking skin because it felt such a part of my life now.

Hicks and Dylan weren't exactly the best house-mates either.

Dylan struggled with being cooped up and Hicks, couldn't stand the way she paced the small apartment, bitching the entire time about basically, everything.

"You live like a fucking pig," Dylan said, lifting a crusty washcloth that smelled like death from the sink. "What the fuck did you do to this?" She dropped it with disgust, wiping her hands on her jeans. "It smells like ass. Dead ass at that."

Hicks glowered from his desk, a bottle of whiskey his equivalent of a morning cup of coffee, retorting, "Well, make yourself useful and clean something then if you're so offended, your highness."

I stuffed down a chuckle at the idea of Dylan being considered delicate in any way. Dylan responded with a look that could kill and left the kitchen to drop onto the sofa with a heavy exhale laced with banked frustration.

The apartment wasn't as small as I originally thought, it was stuffed to the gills with a life spent elsewhere that had nowhere to go. Kinda like us. I tried to imagine Hicks as a responsible man with a wife and an adoring daughter but it was hard to picture the man with the bloodshot eyes and the subtle shake in his hands as anything other than the broken drunk that was trying his damnedest to claw at his redemption, no matter how slim the prospects.

In a way, Hicks wasn't all that different from Dylan and I. We were going up against terrible odds with the same misplaced hope that we might win when everything stacked against us told a different story.

If we were an option on the race track, no one would bet on us.

Dylan swung her attention back to Hicks. The challenging look in her eyes didn't bode well for an easy afternoon. "You ever think about your kid? Like, do you call her or anything?"

Hicks ignored Dylan's question, which was probably smart. Dylan was being self-destructive and itching for a fight, even if it meant getting herself kicked out of the only safe place she had.

"Knock it off, Dylan," I warned.

Hicks returned to his work and an uneasy silence returned. Watching paint dry might be more entertaining but at least I wasn't cold and I didn't have to crap in a bucket. One thing I'd discovered was to appreciate the little things.

I'd thought I already had that on lock but life had a way of kicking you harder when you were down to remind you how fragile your hold on everything was.

"Totally committed to the deadbeat dad life?"

she continued, watching him with a small twist of her lips. "Probably a helluva lot easier than explaining why you're a fucking drunk, huh? Addiction is a bitch."

I rolled my eyes, irritated. "Can you shut your trap? You're just being an asshole for no reason."

"No reason? We're stuck in this garbage can with nothing to do and all he does is drink himself stupid every day and stare at paperwork." To Hicks, she added with a curled lip, "Do you even have cases or are you just staring at blank paper? Seriously, what do you do with your time? How do you pay your bills? I'm bored out of my mind and if something doesn't change, I will burn this place down just to watch the flames."

I held my breath, waiting for Hicks to blow up but he did the opposite. He smiled.

And I think that was more disturbing.

"You think you're a badass?" he asked, lighting a cigarette and inhaling deeply. He spit out a tiny fleck of something, still waiting for Dylan to answer. "Trust me, kid, you ain't shit. You think you're something else because you've seen some things and that sucks for you. I feel for you but you're just a kid at the end of the day and it wouldn't take much to snuff out your life, which is why you're in this position in the first place. You were easy pickings. Think about that for a minute the next minute you want to start poking at someone else's bruises."

I looked to Dylan, wondering if she were going to tell him to go fuck himself but she remained quiet, as if the heart of what he'd just said had punctured that hard shell and she wasn't quite sure what to do about it.

As much as we hated to admit it, we needed the help of adults to fight the adults who were trying to kill us. We were survivors but not necessarily bad-asses, just like Hicks had pointed out.

But that knowledge made me feel small and vulnerable, which was likely the same for Dylan and I knew from experience that Dylan hated feeling either of those things.

Hicks must've felt bad for bringing the hammer down so hard because he sighed and leaned back in his chair, saying, "Yeah, I miss her and no, I don't call her. Better to keep a distance if you're not gonna do nothing but disappoint someone."

Dylan skewed her gaze away with a short nod, murmuring, "Yeah, makes sense."

"Any other burning questions you need to ask?"

Instead of answering, Dylan rose and announced, "I need to take a shit" before disappearing behind the bathroom door.

"You know she's softer than she acts," I said in Dylan's defense. "She just doesn't have any coping skills. She left her dad when she was eleven and she's been on the streets ever since."

"That's a rough gig," Hicks acknowledged with a grunt. "What's the story with her old man?"

"Same as a lot of shitty parents, abusive. When it looked like he was eyeing her boobs a few too many times, Dylan knew what was probably coming and she bailed before he could follow through."

"Takes guts to leave home that young. Most kids aren't that brave."

"Dylan is unlike anyone I've ever met. For that matter, so was Jilly." I fell silent, a wave of grief following. How was it possible that I felt a deep hole inside my heart for a girl I'd barely known? Tana and Jilly were gone and I never really got the chance to know them for real but their loss felt like someone had punched me in the stomach.

"Yeah, you've been served up a shit sandwich, kid," he agreed with another heavy sigh. "The world is full of terrible people all looking to get theirs at the expense of someone else."

"Must've been hard being a cop," I said.

"It had its moments."

"But you miss it, don't you?"

He grabbed the whiskey bottle with a grim, "Every damn day," then lifted the bottle to his lips, as if acknowledging that it was the booze that took everything from him and yet, he couldn't stop himself.

Dylan was right; addiction was a bitch.

As much as I hated to admit, watching Hicks struggle with his addiction and knowing what it'd cost him, made me a tiny bit more sympathetic to Carla, but only by the thinnest margin. I didn't think that if Carla was straight and sober she'd be less of a shit person. The alcohol just enhanced what was already there.

A knock at the door had us both tense. Hicks, even as a drunk, was a formidable ally. He motioned for me to stay put as he grabbed a gun from a hidden spot beneath his desk and approached the door with practiced caution. "Who is it?" he called out.

"It's Pope."

I breathed a sigh of relief, shocked at how fear had instantly drenched my skin and dried up all the spit in my mouth. I rose on shaky legs to grab a glass of water as Hicks let Kerri in.

She entered the apartment holding a bag. Looking my way, she said, "You up for a field trip?" as she tossed the bag to the couch. Curious, I went to the bag and peered inside. I pulled out two wigs and new hoodies. Kerri said, "There are also sunglasses. No sense in making things easy for the fuckers looking for you."

Dylan came from the bathroom, wiping her wet hands on her jeans. "What's that?"

I lifted up the wigs. "Do you prefer blonde or brunette?"

"No way," Dylan grinned in surprise, coming to grab the blonde wig. "I've always wondered if I could pull off this color."

I twirled the cheap brunette mop made of synthetic hair and chuckled. "Guess that means I'm going dark."

"What's this for?" Dylan asked, pulling the wig over her head and tucking the errant dark hair beneath it. I followed suit and did the same. Dylan approved. "You look good as a brunette."

I smiled. "Good to know."

Kerri said, "I need you to come to my office to look at the database. I can't exactly have you waltzing into the station looking like yourselves but the only way to access the system is through the closed network."

"Which means we get to go on a field trip," I said.

Kerri nodded. "Pretty much."

Dylan was ready. "Count me in. This place is giving me hives."

"You sure this is a good idea?" Hicks asked, frowning. "You think it's not going to go unnoticed you bringing in two teens to your office?"

"I'll handle it. Besides, the precinct is practically a ghost town right now. Between vacation scheduling and recent retirements, we've been running a skeleton crew. We're short-staffed as fuck. No one is going to be paying attention to what I'm doing because they've got their own shit to worry about. Caseloads are ridiculous and everyone's just trying to keep their heads above water."

He grunted, appeased by Kerri's answer like he was some overprotective dad or something. I shifted against the odd feeling of having someone care about my welfare. I mean, Lora's dad played the part sometimes but most times it just felt like he was supposed to act that way, not because he really felt concerned about me. Maybe I was just an asshole I didn't know how to accept someone's help but for whatever reason, Hicks' concern felt real.

Dylan, on the other hand, was oblivious and ready to blow the apartment. "Can we stop by and get a burger or something? I'm fucking starved. All this guy has is stale Cheerios and milk that's turning to cottage cheese."

Only a slight exaggeration.

Hicks just shrugged off the criticism, saying, "I told you, I ain't no grand host and this ain't the Hilton."

Kerri shook her head, irritated with Hicks, saying, "Buy some fucking groceries, you idiot. You could use more than whiskey for breakfast, too. I'll be back later this evening."

She didn't mince words or pretend to be anything other than she was and I liked that about her.

I also liked the way she stood her ground, no matter who she was talking to.

It made me wonder what would happen if Kerri came face-to-face with Madame Moirai, whoever the fuck she was.

If and when that ever happened, I hoped Kerri shot the woman's face off.

And I wasn't even sorry for hoping.

I grinned at Kerri, not because I was excited

about a burger, but Kerri didn't know that and just smiled back, saying, "Yeah, we can get a bite to eat before we hit the station" and I followed her out of the apartment with a lighter, if not blood-thirsty, heart.

17

We walked into Kerri's precinct and it smelled like most cop stations — like sweat and old Lysol that hadn't quite given up but would never truly win the germ fight — and true to her word, the place was fairly empty.

"No wonder Madame Moirai gets away with this shit...aren't there any fucking cops doing their jobs?" Dylan muttered, pulling the hoodie more tightly around her neck to retort, "Fills me with a whole lot of confidence that we're gonna win this fight."

I ignored Dylan. I wasn't sure if I was relieved or pissed that the place was empty. All I could think about was all the crimes that weren't being followed up on when I saw the empty desks and phones ringing to nowhere.

"Why is your precinct empty?" I asked.

"Perfect storm of shit. We had a wave of retirements, some lay-offs and some firings and not a lot of heat from the brass to fill the empty seats. Always trying to save a buck. But, this is a temporary problem. Soon enough we'll get some more bodies in here and it'll be a madhouse as usual. In the meantime, this works in our favor."

I didn't argue but I was leaning more toward Dylan's frame of mind. I would've rather seen a bustling precinct than an empty one, even if it meant we were at greater risk of being seen.

Nothing had been easy up to this point, why start now?

Kerri's office gave the word "claustrophobic" a visual representation. There was a desk, crammed with case files two stacks high, a coffee cup that looked as if it hadn't been washed in two years and an old desktop computer that probably had a hamster for an operating system.

Hard to imagine anything but Hepatitis could be found in this place.

Kerri, catching our vibe, said, "Look, don't let the place fool you. Nothing is shiny and new but it gets the job done. Now, come around to this side and take a look at the database."

I thought of something. "Would it be possible to find Tana's grandmother on your database?"

Kerri frowned. "Not in this particular database but DMV search might find a person if they have a valid driver's license. Do you have a name?"

I shook my head, realizing how stupid I sounded. "No. I don't even remember Tana's full name."

Kerri's expression changed to one of resigned understanding. "It's hard to search for a needle in a haystack when you don't even know what the needle looks like."

"We've got bigger issues than finding Tana's grandmother," Dylan groused. "I mean, the woman has dementia, anyway. It's not like she's missing Tana or anything."

"That's fucking harsh," I growled.

Dylan shrugged. "But true."

"Maybe it's stupid and a waste of time but it feels like the only thing we can possibly do for Tana. She cared more about your grandmother than she did herself. She wasn't like us."

"Disposable?" Dylan quipped with a dark look. "You have such a hard-on for that girl and you barely knew her."

"Shut the fuck up, Dylan," I shot back, heat curling the hairs on my neck as my hands curled into tight fists. Sometimes I just wanted to pop the girl in the mouth for the shit that came out of hers like verbal vomit. "Yeah, well, I barely know you or Jilly either. Should I just tell you to fuck off, too?"

"Girls, we don't have time for you to fight about shit we can't control," Kerri interrupted firmly. "Let's get back to the task at hand." To me, she offered, "I'll see if I can ask around. Maybe contact a few in social services and see if I can connect some dots. Sometimes the world is a lot smaller than we think."

It was the best she could do and I accepted. She was right, we had enough on our plate. I shouldn't add more but Tana's ghost rode on my shoulder each night and her memory haunted me when I couldn't sleep.

Of course, now Jilly was there, too.

I blinked back tears. Now wasn't the time to start crying, either. I sniffed back the moisture and refocused. "Okay, let's do this, then."

Kerri opened up a database of registered sex offenders and had us look at page after page of predators that started to blur before my eyes. Frustrated, I said, "The perverts paying to be part of the auction aren't going to be on your database of average run-of-the-mill pervs. These people are protected by their money and connections. There's no way they'd ever end up with a record of their crimes."

Dylan agreed with me, snorting, "This is a waste of time."

"Indulge me," Kerri said, continuing to flip through pages. "Not everyone starts off rich and connected. Maybe we'll get lucky."

"Have we met?" I shot back with derision. "Luck and I have never lived in the same house."

Kerri chuckled at my black humor. "Kid, you and I must've been born under the same star."

I smiled. There was something about Kerri I liked, even wanted to trust but after everything that'd gone down, there was always that niggling voice that warned me not to let my guard down for anyone.

If I wasn't careful, I'd end up as closed off as Dylan.

Suddenly, Dylan stiffened and pointed to the screen. "That person...I recognize her." She looked to me for confirmation. "Remember? She's the ugly-ass bitch who gave us the enema."

My eyes widened in agreement. "Holy shit. Dylan is right." I peered a little more closely to read her legal name. "Regina Baker. The name's too unassuming for a bitch like her. She was a monster. Now that I think about it, I think she enjoyed the pain we were in."

"I'd remember that face anywhere."

"Yeah, she was easy to remember."

"How so?" Kerri asked, interested.

"Because the rest of Madame Moirai's staff were...I don't know, like us, younger and good-looking."

Dylan nodded. "This woman looked like she hit the broad side of the ugly truck."

I nodded, adding, "And she was meaner than a junk-yard dog."

Kerri clicked on Regina Baker's details and read them out loud. "Regina Ann Baker, 43, of Brooklyn Heights, convicted of lewd and lascivious acts with a minor under fourteen. Sentenced to Bayview but released for good behavior after only a year." Kerri frowned, clicking her tongue against her teeth in thought. "That's some bullshit."

"So child molesters get passes for good behavior?" I asked, disgusted. "People who fuck with kids are the worst manipulators."

"And the prison justice system is full of fucking cheats and liars," Dylan quipped.

A thought came to me. "What if Madame Moirai pulled some strings to get Regina out early?"

"But why? Like you said, she doesn't seem to fit the profile of those who work for The Avalon," Kerri said.

I snapped my fingers, remembering, "She hired guards, too. Real sons-of-bitches with a cruel streak. Maybe that's the qualification she was looking for in Regina. You gotta have mean-ass dogs to guard your property, right?"

Kerri liked where I was going. "That's a pretty solid theory," she said, moving out of the predator page and into a different database. "Baker's criminal history should be here, too."

She accessed a file and it bloomed on the screen. "She's got priors for disorderly conduct, assault, drugs, theft...Jesus, she's a real peach. Habitual, career criminal with a side of deviant."

"Sounds about right," Dylan muttered. "She was a real bitch."

Kerri wanted to know more. "What else do you remember about the guards? Were they wearing any kind of identifying company uniform?"

Dylan deferred to me, saying, "I didn't get a good look at them. I was locked in my room the whole time but Nicole got more face-time with them."

"Yeah," I said, remembering the psychopath who

most definitely would've raped me if his guard buddy hadn't stepped in to stop him. I tried hard to remember details. "One of the guard's name was Darryl," I shared. "I overheard a conversation between the three guards in the kitchen when I was sneaking around trying to free the girls." I swallowed at the memory, wincing. "Darryl wanted to rape Dylan but the other guard stopped him, saying, his DNA couldn't be found on the body, implying that they knew all along that Dylan and Jilly weren't leaving."

"That fucker," Dylan muttered with barely concealed rage. She knew exactly who I was talking about. "If he would've tried, I'd have bit his fucking dick off."

I nodded. I would've done the same. "They didn't expect Dylan to make it through the night. They said the last girl who came in as injured as Dylan, died before morning. She bled out."

Kerri looked at Dylan with fresh concern. "What were the extent of your injuries?"

Dylan shrugged. "I dunno. It's not like I had a doctor looking me over. I was pissing blood for a few days and I think I got a few toes broken and possibly this finger," she said, as she tried to bend her pinky only to immediately stop with a wince. "Yeah, still hurts like a bitch but I'm not pissing blood anymore so that's a good sign, right?"

"Likely kidney or liver damage," Kerri mused, shaking her head as she gestured for Dylan to let her check her pinky. After a quick look, she agreed, "It was broken but it seems to be healing. However, unless you can get a doc to break it and reset it properly, it's never going to bend right."

"I got bigger problems than a fucked up pinky finger," Dylan said.

Kerri agreed but said, "If you start peeing blood again, you tell me. Got it?"

"Yeah, sure," Dylan answered with a noncommittal shrug. She wasn't used to people giving a shit about her well-being, even more so than me. Gesturing to the computer, she asked, "So, now you have a name. You gonna go pick her up or something?"

"I don't have anything to charge her with but I can drop in and ask a few questions."

"What do you mean? She knows Madame Moirai is killing teen girls. Bring her in and make her tell you how to find that awful bitch," I said with a scowl. "Torture her or something. Make her talk."

"Contrary to what you may think, cops aren't allowed to torture potential suspects," Kerri responded dryly. "Not that we haven't been tempted...but yeah, really frowned upon by the higher-ups."

"Fuck them," Dylan said, stabbing a finger at the screen "that cunt tortured us and enjoyed it. And, now that I know she's a fucking pervert, too, she probably jacked off after having her grubby hands all over our pussies."

I shuddered, feeling a little sick. Dylan wasn't wrong, though. Madame Moirai would've had to hire people who had a vested interest in keeping their mouths shut. What better way to hire from the cesspool to ensure protection?

For that matter, Asshole Guard Darryl hadn't been able to get his hands on me but who's to say he hadn't put his hands on some other girl when his boss wasn't looking?

"I didn't say I wasn't going to pay her a visit," Kerri said, setting us straight firmly. "Look, there's protocol for a reason. Baker is small potatoes. Squeezing her prematurely isn't going to do anything but scare away the real players. Baker is a nothing day player, if you catch my drift. Let me see what kind of pressure I can put on her and then we'll go from there. In the meantime, let's keep looking through the database and see if you see any more of Madame Moirai's employees."

It seemed an innocuous word for the henchmen and women Madame Moirai employed. They were rotten to their core, oozing pestilence from their soul. Maybe that was Madame Moirai's gift, she could sense the corruption or the weakness in another human being, giving her an advantage when needing to refill her ranks.

"I set fire to the auction house. There should be a record of the fire, somewhere. The house was huge. It would've taken a full fire department to put it out," I told Kerri. "Maybe you could ask around the local departments upstate. We were about an hour from the city."

"How do you know you were an hour?" Kerri asked.

"Because that's how long it took to get back once we boosted a car."

Dylan shot me a glance as if to say, *shut the fuck up about the crimes we committed*, but we had to start trusting people if we were going to beat Madame Moirai. To her credit, Kerri didn't flinch at the admission.

"Do you think you would remember how to get back to the place where you stole the car?" she asked.

I shared a look with Dylan before slowly nodding.

"Good. Then, tomorrow, we're going on a field trip."

I swallowed, overcome with an irrational urge to start crying. The auction house was gone. I burned it to the ground.

But the idea of going anywhere near that place... made me want to shit myself.

Fuck, some bad-ass I turned out to be.

18

The next morning, I threw up and had diarrhea. I exited the bathroom, feeling shaky and weak, to find Dylan regarding me with knowing commiseration. Running away from the scene of the crime had been easy, returning felt like walking into the flames of hell.

"We don't have to go," Dylan said.

"If we don't want to keep running and hiding in the shadows, we do," I countered, wiping my mouth. "I'll be fine. I just needed to purge my system."

Dylan nodded in grim agreement. "I was up before you. I don't have anything left in my system."

Hicks exited his bedroom looking like warmed over shit but at least he was sober. Or mostly sober. He ignored us and went straight to the coffee pot, poured a hot steaming cup and started drinking. We were starting to understand his routine. He drank himself stupid until night, crashed hard, and then the next morning jumpstarted his engine with hard-core black coffee that tasted like it'd been scraped off the bottom of a jet engine and then, he started in with the booze by mid-morning.

But today, he'd have to go without his crutch because Kerri didn't tolerate his bullshit. She wanted him sober if he was going with us and she didn't mess around with excuses.

He also didn't argue with her.

"Be ready in five," he said, his voice thick with morning gravel, then disappeared back into his room with his cup of joe.

"The man will be dead within a year or two if he doesn't change his lifestyle," Dylan said. "Have you ever actually seen him eat food? He lives off coffee, cigarettes, and booze. Recipe for a heart attack or stroke."

I agreed. Unlike Dylan, who felt little empathy for most people, I felt bad for his daughter. His addiction had stolen a father and a husband, who, at one time, might've been a really good guy.

I'd never known my dad. Dylan's dad had been a sick fuck. Jilly hadn't shared much about her parents but they must've been pretty fucking bad if the state had cut off all legal ties to Jilly when they were small. The system was overloaded with kids in need of homes. If they could keep the kids with the parents, they did. Even if the parents were pretty much shit.

So that goes to show just how had Jilly's parents had been.

My eyes watered. *Goddamn it, don't think about Jilly.* Now wasn't the time. Sniffing up my clogged sinuses, I wiped at my face and said, "Maybe he can turn his life around. You never know."

Dylan chuckled as if I were stupid, saying, "Yeah, sure. And I fart rainbows."

I knew for a fact, she definitely didn't fart rainbows. I chuckled despite her dry remark. "As always, keeping it real, right?" I said.

"Always and forever, baby girl."

At that, I laughed. It was absurd and hilarious at the same time but I needed the laugh.

Hicks opened his door, fully dressed and looking semi-human. "Let's go, Kerri is waiting downstairs."

"Shotgun," Dylan called out.

Hicks didn't even break his stride as he walked down the hallway, saying, "The fuck you are" and Dylan grinned because she liked nothing more than to be a pain in Hicks' backside.

An older black SUV idled on the curb, waiting for us. Black vehicles gave me the heebie-jeebies now but as I approached I saw Kerri wave to us and I relaxed. Just as I knew she would, Dylan tried to push past Hicks to the front passenger seat and Hicks grabbed her by the scruff of her neck and moved her aside in a smooth movement to the backseat.

"Fucker," she muttered around a half-hidden smile and climbed inside next to me.

I started to smile at Kerri but the expression on her face didn't bode well for good news. "What?" I asked, apprehensive.

"Seems someone is interested in finding you," she said, pulling a piece of paper with an outdated picture of my face and my details. I took the paper between nerveless fingers, shocked at seeing myself listed as "missing." I looked at Kerri. "Who filed this?"

"Apparently, your mother."

Shock dropped my jaw. "Are you sure? My mother doesn't give two shits about me." Another thought came to me. "Maybe Madame Moirai had someone pretend to be my mother."

To that, Kerri produced her cell and pulled up a video. Carla appeared on a grainy, recorded feed from social media, playing the distraught mother, pleading for her daughter's return or for information on my whereabouts.

Dylan peered at the video, saying, "You kinda look like her."

I glared. "Fuck you." I returned to the video. "When was this recorded?"

"Yesterday. She posted on Facebook Live."

"My mom doesn't use Facebook," I said. "The woman can barely operate her cell phone," adding with a derisive snort, "She's usually too drunk."

"Well, she seems to have figured it out now," Kerri said. "There's also a GoFundMe page for her."

"What? Why?"

"According to the page, she lost her job because she was spending so much time searching for you and now she needs money to cover basic expenses."

I knew it was all bullshit. My mom wasn't out there looking for her lost daughter. This was her new con and she was using me to make a buck.

I didn't know why it hurt. I should've seen it coming but I guess I hadn't given Carla much thought. Dylan took the cell out of my hand and gave it back to Kerri. "I take it back — you don't look anything alike. That bitch is ugly as fuck."

And there it was, that sudden, fierce support that

Dylan was famous for and in that moment, I needed it so bad. I nodded and spoke around the lump in my throat. "Yeah, well, Carla has always been looking for her ten minutes of fame. I guess she figured this was it."

"You're not going to tell Carla where Nicole is, right?" Dylan asked in a sharp tone. "You know her mother's a piece of shit. Madame Moirai could've easily gotten to her, offering up a fat payout for Nicole's head on a platter. We can't trust anything that comes out of that whore's trap."

"I'm not telling her anything," Kerri calmed us both. "But it does complicate things. An official report will put you on everyone's radar. You're going to need to keep an eye on your surroundings."

"Same story, different day," I quipped, finding my footing again. "Are you going to question Carla?"

"Yeah, I want to see what she knows, poke at her a bit and see what pops out," Kerri said.

"I'd do anything to be a fly on the wall when that happens," I said.

"Not a bad idea," Kerri said, surprising me. "I could wire up and give you a headset to listen in. Might be useful to hear with your own ears the story she's peddling."

"That's fucking brilliant," Dylan said, grinning. "Like real spy shit and everything."

Kerri smiled. "Yeah, something like that. All right, buckle up, we're going on a road trip."

"I hope you brought snacks," I said, leaning back and clicking my seatbelt, noting that the entire time, Hicks hid from the sunlight behind pitch-black sunglasses, resting his head against his fingers and his elbow propped against the windowpane. I was pretty sure he was asleep already.

Kerri nudged him awake, gesturing to his seatbelt. "Safety first, motherfucker."

"Jesus-fucking-Christ, Kerri," he grumbled but grudgingly pulled the strap across his chest, clicking it in place. "Satisfied?"

There was a fascinating dysfunction between those two that was hard to look away from. Seeing as I'd never had a mom and dad present, only Carla, I imagined this was what having parents felt like.

Not in a normal situation, of course. My guess was that normal parents weren't alcoholics or workaholics with intimacy issues but maybe I was way off and that was normal because the whole world was a mixed bag of fucked-up colored candy.

We cleared the city and hit the freeway heading

upstate. Everything looked different in the day, when you weren't running for your lives.

I mean, still running, but I felt a smidge safer with Kerri and Hicks both packing heat. I wish we would've had the foresight to grab the gun from Badger's place but we'd hightailed it out of that place so fast I think we left our shadows behind.

Speaking of...I leaned over to Dylan, asking, "Have you heard from Badger lately?"

"No."

"Seems kinda weird, doesn't it?"

She shrugged. "He's not really a talker. Besides, life doesn't stop for him just because of a few bodies lying around."

That was a terrible thought. I regarded Dylan with curiosity. We had time to kill. Kerri was listening to classic rock and Hicks was snoring.

"Tell me about Nova," I said.

"Like what?" Dylan asked, wary. "Like what she looked like and shit like that?"

"Whatever. Tell me what you liked about her. What made her special?"

"I already told you. She took me in when I had no one."

Dylan wasn't an open book on anything

personal. She guarded that stuff like a dragon hoarding gold.

"You loved her," I said.

She shrugged. "Maybe, yeah, I guess so. I mean, she was family. She was all I had."

For the girl who believed in no one and didn't trust easily, Nova had become the one person she would've died for. Why else would she have knowingly chased after Madame Moirai to find her?

"You know, I realized something the other day... each of you took the deal for noble reasons, except me. My decision had been purely selfish. I just wanted to get away from Carla and start fresh."

"I did it for the money," Dylan corrected me but I didn't buy it. I already knew Dylan better than I had a right to know anyone. Trauma had a way of bonding people with super glue but it also laid bare all the tender spots we tried to hide. Dylan exhaled, looking away. "Well, the money would've been a bonus, I guess. I just wanted to bring Nova home."

"It wasn't your fault," I told her. "I know you blame yourself for not telling Badger about Nova's deal but how could you have known how badly it was going to go? None of us had a clue. We were duped. Your only crime was ignoring the same voice we all ignored."

"Yeah, maybe."

"Badger said something to me a few weeks ago... that he'd hoped Nova would go to college, get out of the life they were in. Did he ever mention that to you?"

Dylan shook her head but didn't appear hurt. "College was never for me."

"Why not? You're pretty damn smart."

"Too many rules. Too many expectations. I don't like feeling caged in."

I never would've known just to look at her that Dylan was an anarchist free-spirit with a hidden heart of gold. Loyalty was infused in Dylan's DNA. She'd die for anyone she considered part of her inner circle.

A lot like Jilly.

And Jilly had died for us both.

God, I missed her annoying voice. I missed her laughter at weird moments and the strange, slightly sociopathic bent of her logic that always made me a little worrisome about her mental health.

I chuckled, only to stop the tears from starting. Dylan sensed my energy change and somehow knew it was about Jilly.

"I miss her, too," she admitted, staring down at her hands, interlacing her fingers together and fidgeting. "I mean...as much as you can miss a stranger, you know?"

True, we'd only known each other a short time but our circumstances had accelerated our bond to an almost psychic level. Shame pricked my thoughts when I realized I felt closer to Dylan and Jilly than I did to Lora who I'd known since I was a little kid.

What I knew to be true, was that I would die for Dylan if I had to...and she would do the same for me.

And neither of us had seen that coming.

19

Since Dylan drove the car when we bailed she gave Kerri instructions where to turn and what off-ramp to take. Before too long we were out of the city and flanked by tall trees, snow covering the ground from the recent storm. The air had a bite to it, like a meat locker on turbo freeze, reminding me of the night we ran from the auction house.

We ran without shoes for our feet, just those stupid, thin, house slippers that hateful bitch Olivia had given us along with our pajamas. Knowing what I knew now, I wondered if they recycled the pajamas after they snuffed out the girl in them.

I tried to remember how many slabs were in the morgue. All I could distinctly remember was Tana's battered body beneath the sheet. Actually, no, that wasn't true. I could still smell the sharp chemical scent from the embalming liquids as if that smell were permanently lodged in my nose.

"There," Dylan said, pointing between Kerri and Hicks to the house that provided us sanctuary when we needed it most. Her voice sounded thick and strangled. "That's the one."

The house was exactly as we remembered. Not that it'd been all that long since we were there but it also felt like a lifetime ago. The last time we were here, Jilly was with us.

Kerri slowly pulled into the driveway, motioning for us to wait in the car while she knocked on the door. We held our breath. My heartbeat painfully against my chest. The front door opened and a woman appeared — older, probably retirement age — wrapping her cardigan more firmly around her shoulders, peering at Kerri in question. We couldn't hear what Kerri was saying but the woman seemed to relax.

Hicks removed his sunglasses and his gaze roamed the sleepy neighborhood. "Mostly vacation homes, looks like. Bunch of boomers looking to supplement their retirement."

"Do you think that's the homeowner?" I asked,

feeling bad for the money we stole and basically everything we took from them. "She looks nice."

Hicks shrugged because he didn't know and didn't want to speculate. Kerri finished and headed back, the woman returning inside.

Kerri climbed back into the car to report what she heard. "Someone reported the break-in. The homeowners are staying temporarily until they can hire a full-time caretaker for the rest of the winter until it's time to start renting it out again."

"She looked nice," I said.

"Yeah," Kerri said, distracted as she pulled out of the driveway and back onto the road. "She said they had to do some renovations because of the damage. I thought you said you just took essentials?"

I frowned. "What damage? We were careful not to break anything. We just took clothes, cash and food. That's it. And we slept in one bed because it was freezing and we showered in the bathroom. What kind of damage did she say was done?"

"Holes in the walls, trashed furniture, broken glass."

"Fuck, we didn't do that," Dylan said, indignant. "What a bunch of fuckers, claiming we did that shit for the insurance money. They're getting a whole house makeover and claiming we did the damage."

"We also stole their car," I added, but agreed with Dylan. "They're fucking opportunists. Now I don't feel so bad about stealing from them."

Kerri smiled but she seemed to be chewing on something else in her head. "So, you found this place in the dark and ran on foot from the auction house so the auction house can't be far from this little neighborhood."

"Yeah, but like you said, it was dark. I wasn't exactly looking at landmarks. We were just running like our lives depended on it because it did," I said. "I couldn't even tell you what town this is."

"According to GPS, we're in Esterdell, a very small, sleepy historic town without a lot of permanent residents but it's a booming tourist trap during the summer months, which explains the clump of vacation homes," Kerri said. "But seeing as it's so small, there ought to be someone who reported a mansion on fire. We need to swing by the local police department and see if I can get some professional courtesy." To Hicks, she said, "You can drop me off and then you take the girls around and see if something doesn't jog their memory."

Hicks offered up a grim agreement but he looked as sour as a curdled stomach. They pulled up to the police department, a quaint place that looked like something plucked from a movie set as if no real crime happened around here, and Hicks took the driver's seat. Before leaving us, Kerri revealed a rare show of support, grasping Hicks' arm, saying, "You got this" and left.

I waited until we were driving away to pepper him with questions. "What did that mean? You got *what?*"

Dylan agreed, interested as well. "Sounds personal. What's going on?"

"You're right — it's *personal.*"

"As Badger would say, that doesn't sit well with me. You gave up 'personal' when you agreed to take this job," Dylan said. "What if whatever this secret of yours puts us in danger? Ever think of that?"

I squared up my gaze, agreeing with Dylan. Secrets had a bad way of biting us in the ass and we weren't about to take chances.

When Hicks realized neither one of us was going to let him off the hook, he relented with his signature bad humor. "Jesus fucking Christ, you're like a pair of hound dogs on a scent. Relax. It's nothing like that."

"Yeah? So spill it if it's no big deal," I said.

He exhaled with a growl, "I used to live around this area. Hard being back."

I blinked in sudden understanding. "Does your kid live here?"

"Close enough."

"Man, I don't know why I just assumed that they lived in the city. So, you kept your family in Quaintsville while you roamed the hard streets, huh? No wonder you're an alcoholic. Hard to keep those worlds apart," Dylan said, shaking her head as if amused by his pain. "Must suck being back."

"It does."

"But that means you know the area pretty well?" I asked, moving onto information that benefited us.

"Well enough."

"Good. You might've mentioned that point earlier."

"Why do you think I came along? For fucking funsies? A lovely day trip with three bossy as fuck females and no fucking booze to calm my nerves? Yeah, not my idea of a good time."

"I thought you came to hang out with Kerri, actually," I said, being honest. "You seem to have a thing for her."

"Bullshit," he muttered. "There ain't nothing between Kerri and I so don't go trying to play Matchmaker, got it?"

I ignored him. "Not for nothing, I think she likes

you, too. Did you have a thing or something when you were working together? An office affair?"

"No, we did not," he said pointedly.

"But you wanted to," I said.

"Drop it, kid."

I smiled at his quick defensive tone. I knew people pretty well. I could tell when they were trying to hide something. *Well, usually.* The whole situation with Madame Moirai had thrown me from my game. *Speaking of...*"Why would Madame Moirai go to all the trouble of embalming the bodies of dead auction girls if she's just going to get rid of them somewhere?"

Hicks, relieved to talk about anything not related to his feelings, ruminated on my question, finally agreeing that it was odd, answering gruffly, "Embalmed bodies are preserved. Typically, murderers like their victims to be unidentifiable. Are you sure it was embalming fluid and not a lye solution?"

"Positive. I remember a few things from school."

"Maybe there's a graveyard somewhere filled with auction girls," Dylan said.

"Again, why preserve the bodies? Even if they had a dedicated area for their victims, it doesn't make sense that they would preserve them. Preserving the bodies is for several purposes, containing the spread of disease from the dead bodies, and providing the option for loved ones to do a final viewing before burial."

"Something tells me Madame Moirai ain't holding funerals for the girls she kills," I said.

"Not likely," Hicks agreed, shaking his head. "That doesn't add up."

"Maybe that's why they've been getting away with killing girls...because they've found a way around the obvious," I said.

Dylan nodded. "Ain't no one saying that Madame Moirai ain't smart. She's probably the best damn con artist and businesswoman I've ever seen. Except no one has ever actually *seen* her."

"How do you know Madame Moirai is a woman?" Hicks asked.

"We don't," I admitted. "All we know is that everyone who works for her *or him* fears their wrath if they screw up. Even the sociopathic guard had enough sense to back off when threatened with Madame Moirai's displeasure. It's like Madame Moirai was the evil queen of human trafficking and no one was going to dare cross her or else risk ending up in the ground, too."

"Takes time to build a reputation like that," he

mused. "And lots of money to start up the operation with connections like she's got."

"She's got all the right connections. Corrupt motherfucker," I muttered. "She sent real killers to take us out. She wasn't taking any chances. The only thing working in our favor is that she keeps underestimating our will to survive."

"At first glance, seems a bit of an overkill, sending assassins to take out three teens," Hicks said. "She must really think you're a liability if she's willing to go that far."

Except we didn't all make it out. Maybe when it was all said and done, we didn't make out alive either.

It was a sobering reality. I shared a look with Dylan. We didn't want to die. I needed to focus on something other than my own demise. I focused on the road, the landscape, anything that might jog our memory of that night.

But after a good forty-five minutes of driving up one road and down another without success, I sank back against the seat, chewing on the bitterness of inevitable defeat.

"Who the fuck are we kidding?" I said. "It was pitch black outside when we ran and it's not like we were paying attention to anything but surviving.

Nothing looks familiar to me." Dylan nodded, agreeing in frustrated silence. I pinched the bridge of nose to keep from crying. "It's like pushing a fucking rock up a hill wearing roller skates. There's no way to win."

"That's the whole point," Dylan said quietly. "If we win, they lose and they're not going to let that happen."

"Hold up," Hicks said, trying to make us feel better "everyone makes mistakes. Even criminal masterminds. I've seen it a million times. Arrogance will trip up even the most Type A motherfucker around. I don't care who the fuck this Madame Moirai is...she isn't perfect. Somewhere along the way, mistakes were made and we're going to find them. So knock that shit off. No quitting, you hear me?"

It was a shit excuse for a pep talk but the kernel of his message took root. He had a point. No one was perfect. The cleaning crew had overlooked the bobby pins stuck in the carpet of my room, which had enabled me to pick the lock. The guards had been more interested in getting drunk and playing cards than doing their jobs, which had enabled me to sneak around the auction house and free Jilly and Dylan.

Madame Moirai had sucked Dylan into her

scheme without realizing that Dylan would be a fucking nightmare to contain.

I released a pent up breath, realizing something. "Hicks is right. Think of Madame Moirai in terms of a giant corporation with many moving parts...eventually, even the most well-oiled machine breaks down somewhere. We just have to find the broken cogs. If we can find the weakest links, we can use them to climb the chain."

Hicks gave me a crooked grin that almost looked like pride as he said, "You'd make a good cop someday, kid. You've got the head for it."

"Yeah, right," I murmured. *Me? A fucking cop? Not likely.* But it was nice to hear someone say something positive about me that didn't come with strings attached. I pushed a chunk of hair behind my ear, adding a quick, "Thanks" and I left it at that.

Maybe today wasn't going to give us the big breaks we were hoping for but it wasn't all for nothing either.

As it turned out...Kerri might've just found one of the weaker links — and it would feel fucking fantastic to squeeze the truth out of that motherfucker.

20

Kerri climbed into the passenger side, her cheeks pinked as if she'd spent some time walking around in the cold.

"What'd you find?" I asked. "Was there a fire reported at a big mansion in the area?"

"Yes," Kerri answered, rubbing her hands together "but it was reported to be a kitchen fire that didn't require a full detail."

I drew back. "A kitchen fire? What the fuck? I started the fire in the basement."

"Right," Kerri confirmed with a self-satisfied smile as if she were about to reveal something epic. "So I took a stroll down to the fire department and talked to the fire chief. Nice guy. Real happy to help. He double-checked the report from the on-duty captain, it was logged as a kitchen fire and put out without incident. No one, aside from a few staff, were in the house at the time of the blaze and everyone evacuated safely."

I was confused. "That's all wrong," I protested, looking to Dylan. "Holy fuck, do they own this fucking town, lock, stock, and barrel? Jesus fucking Christ." That last part was muttered between a sudden spring of tears choking my throat. "What are we supposed to do if they've got the local yokels to lie for them and falsify reports?"

"Hold up," Kerri said, "there's more. Yes, the chief confirmed what was on the report but he doesn't have reason to question a report on something as simple as a fire in the kitchen. I wasn't surprised that he didn't question the report. For him, it was less than nothing to think about. But just as I was leaving, a little frustrated at the dead end, an engineer motioned to get my attention and I followed him outside. Once out of earshot, he told me something that I can definitely work with."

I wiped my eyes. "Yeah? Like what?"

Dylan leaned forward, her eyes hard. "Yeah....like what?" she repeated.

"Engineer Ripp seemed on edge, anxiety rippling off him like waves of summer heat...he had something he had to get off his chest and after assuring him that he was doing the right thing and that it was just between us, he sang like a fucking canary. In fact, he was so goddamned relieved to get it off his chest it felt like a fucking confessional. I didn't know if he expected me to give him a few 'Hail Marys' for his trouble."

Hicks caught on before us. "He was working that night. He saw something that wasn't exactly on the report?" he surmised.

Kerri nodded. "The fire had pretty much destroyed the basement area and some areas of the upper level but they managed to suppress the fire without any injuries and returned to the station. However, Ripp happened to catch an accidental look at the report right before it was filed and it sure as hell didn't state the facts as he remembered them."

"Like how?" Dylan asked.

"Well, the first thing, was, about the location of the fire. It was clear it hadn't originated in the kitchen and the strong chemical smell indicated an accelerant but there was no mention of that in the report."

"He said there were staff? That means Olivia must've been in the house when the fire started," I said.

"Too bad she didn't die," Dylan said without a hint of apology. "Fucking cunt can burn in hell for all I care."

I shared Dylan's feelings. I hated Madame Moirai for her part but Olivia's role felt so much more insidious. She knew the degradation of being an auction girl and yet, she continued to feed girls to the beast knowing that they were likely going to die before they saw any money.

Maybe it was savage but I didn't care that Olivia had once been a victim. People made choices. If we were going to be judged for making the choice to sign on the dotted line, Olivia had to reconcile herself to the consequence of selling her fucking soul to the devil.

"So what now? Is there a list of the people in the house? Wouldn't that have been in the report? If we can get a hold of the staff in the house we can start putting the pressure on them to get to Madame Moirai."

Kerri shook her head. "I got something better." All of us were hanging on Kerri's intel. "I got the name of the *captain* who wrote the report."

"Sounds like we need to pay a visit to this captain," Hicks said, smiling for the first time. "Nice fucking work, Pope."

"So why'd this engineer rat out his captain?" Dylan asked, wary. "Ain't nothing for free. He got beef with his boss? What if this is a trap or something? Madame Moirai had to know that we'd start asking questions about the fire."

"Under most circumstances, I'd have the same reservations as you but I have a sixth sense about people and I know when they're lying. This kid was uncomfortable with what he'd discovered. Like, he just walked in on his hero fucking the dog. A good kid like that is going to struggle with finding out something bad about his mentor. Sometimes the idealizations of youth work in your favor when you're chasing a case down."

"What's the captain's name?" I asked.

"Darryl Farroni," Kerri answered.

A cold wave of revulsion washed over me. Could it be the same repulsive guard who'd been more than happy to put his grubby hands all over me when no one was looking? But how was that possible? I couldn't imagine Asshole Darryl being anyone's version of a hero. "Why would a fire captain moonlight as a security guard for a shady operation?" I asked, questioning if it could be the same guy. "That doesn't make a lot of sense. Don't fire captains make bank on their own?"

"In the city, yeah sure. In rural areas where the fire department isn't much more than a volunteer operation during the winter...not so much. A lot of firefighters and cops take side gigs to make ends meet in the offseason," Hicks said. "It's one of the reasons I worked in the city but my family lived upstate. Better environment, better money."

"How suburban of you," Dylan quipped. "Okay, so let's go get this bastard and break his thumbs or something until he squeals."

"No one is breaking thumbs," Kerri said. "I'll bring him in for questioning so everything is by the book. We need to be able to build a case."

"Screw that," Dylan said, growing angry. "They don't play by the fucking rules. What makes you think that just because you're trying to play fair that they will too? You said he hasn't been around for a few days? My money is on one of two options: he's dead or he's gone. Madame Moirai doesn't like loose ends, remember? What's a fucking crooked piece of shit like Darryl Farroni considered? Pretty fucking loose, if you ask me."

I had to agree with Dylan. "We're already here... we should just see if he's around. I mean, you don't need a warrant to be neighborly, right? Just make up some bullshit so you can look him in the eye and see if he's lying through his fucking teeth."

"And then fucking put a bullet in his gut," Dylan said as if that made perfect sense. "Gut wounds take longer to bleed out if you do it right." Asshole Darryl had been pretty brutal with Dylan, too. Kerri better watch Dylan or the girl might just grab Kerri's gun and do the job herself.

"Dylan, calm the fuck down," Kerri instructed, shaking her head. "I get that you want him dead and for good reason, if it's the same guy but there's the right way and the fucked up to do things. Trust me on this."

"Why? Because you've dealt with psychopathic secret organizations that traffic kids to rich pervs before? No, you haven't. You keep tip-toeing around the ethics and you're going to end up dead, too. Sorry, but that's just the facts. Madame Moirai is a vicious cunt and she's not going to stop at putting down anyone who gets in her way."

Kerri fell silent, as if digesting Dylan's prophecy. The tension in the cab felt thick and heavy like one of my Gran's old musty quilts she kept in the closet with the towels. "Even if you're right, you still gotta be smart, kid," Kerri said.

But Hicks seemed to like Dylan's idea. "Stay

with me a minute...wouldn't be too hard to get his address and do a quick drive-by, check out the lay of the land. Call it a welfare check. From what the engineer said he hasn't seen him in a few days right? Sounds like he might be in danger. That's probable cause at the very least."

"This isn't my jurisdiction," Kerri reminded Hicks. "All I've got is professional courtesy. If I want to start making house calls under police business, I have to ring the local PD to assist."

"Yeah, and let whoever is on the fucking payroll know that we're onto them? Sure, sounds like a great plan," Dylan quipped with disgust. "Might as well put a fucking bell around our necks so they can hear us coming."

Hicks nodded in agreement, gesturing to Dylan. "Kid's gotta point, Kerri."

Kerri wasn't amused with his input or the fact that everyone in the car seemed to disagree with her. "Look I know it's been a while since you've been an *actual* cop but in case you haven't noticed we have two minors in the car. What if shit goes down? I'm not taking the chance that Dylan and Nicole might get hurt."

Hicks lit a cigarette, shaking out the match and blowing the smoke out the window. "Look I don't want them getting hurt either but they already have someone trying to kill them so I say we go check out this fucker and see what we can find out. It's not like we have all the time in the world to play things by the book."

Kerri's expression darkened. "You may not find value in following the rules but those of us still on the job understand that we can't just do what we want to do when we want to do it."

"Oh hell, Kerri. Take the stick out of your ass for just a second and listen to what I'm trying to say. We're not gonna do anything but talk to the guy. Where's the harm in that?"

"This is a shit idea," Kerri growled but she was wavering.

"Most great ideas always look like shit on paper," Hicks said. "Stop thinking like an administrator and be a fucking detective. You and I both know intuition isn't something you can teach. Listen to your gut."

"My gut says you're a fucking menace to my career and if I keep listening to you, I'm probably fucked."

"Okay, ignore your gut," Hicks returned with an almost charming grin.

Kerri exhaled with a glower. "I swear to God if

anything happens to these girls I'm gonna kill you myself."

Hicks smirked. "Well honey, you'd have to get in line there's a long list of women that want to put me into the ground, starting with my ex-wife. Let's go." He turned the key and we hit the road again while Kerri found Darryl Farroni's home address.

Watching Kerri and Hicks interact was nothing short of a trip in a surreal world that felt oddly comforting. I mean, they're dysfunctional as fuck but I guess that was my comfort zone. I was relieved that Hicks talked Kerri into following up this lead. I was itching to finally connect some dots but I was also terrified of seeing that psychopathic man again.

What gave me courage was knowing that both Kerri and Hicks would blow that motherfucker's head off if he threatened me or Dylan...even if it meant breaking the rules.

21

The house, small and off the beaten path, was a little run-down but at one time had probably been really cute, like something from a postcard. Snow pressed on the aging wooden fence lining the yard and the arbor hanging over the entrance was losing the battle against time, sagging dangerously.

Either Asshole Darryl had inherited the place from his family or he'd purchased a fixer-upper with the intent to put some sweat equity in to raise the value to sell.

My money was on the inheritance. Asshole Darryl didn't seem the enterprising type. Going by my experiences with the shit-stain, Darryl had been more of an opportunist, getting what he could get when the getting was good. I felt bad for anyone who'd ever had to call him a blood relation.

"Someone isn't really into home improvement," Dylan quipped from the backseat, earning a nod from me.

"All right, this is how it's gonna go down," Kerri instructed in a stern tone "you two stay here in the car. Hicks and I will check this guy out."

"You're not going to know if it's him or not if we don't go with you," I argued.

"Yeah, and if it is him, he's going to recognize you right away. Think with your head, not your heart. Emotion gets people killed," Kerri admonished.

I looked to Hicks for back up but he seemed to agree.

Sullen, I slumped against the seat, folding my arms across my chest. "Fine, whatever."

Dylan was suspiciously compliant, simply nodding as if she thought Kerri's plan was brilliant, which immediately told me she was up to something.

Sure enough, as soon as Kerri and Hicks were out of the car and at the front door, she motioned for me to quietly follow.

It was hard to move like a ninja in snow, each crunching step sounding louder than the next, but we swung around to the back of the house so we could get a good visual. From where we were, we could see inside the house and holy shit, the man was a terrible housekeeper.

Or else, someone had come through his place with a wrecking ball and a grudge to settle.

Dylan nudged me, pointing. Someone was lying on the carpet, a dark pool beneath him. "That fucker is dead," Dylan said, shaking her head. "C'mon, we gotta tell Hicks and Kerri."

We ran to the front of the house, just as Kerri was poised to knock again. Dylan said, a little out of breath, "Don't bother. Whoever lives here is dead. We saw him through the back window."

Kerri frowned, going around to a better vantage point to peek through a grungy window. "Sure enough, that's a body," she confirmed grimly. To us, she said with mild exasperation, "Do you ever stay fucking put?"

Both Dylan and I shook our heads. No point in lying, right? Besides, it was a rhetorical question. Like she really expected us to sit in the car like a bunch of toddlers? *Yeah, sure.* The whole 'running for our lives' situation had dampened our already weak ability to listen to authority.

"Do we call it in?" Kerri asked Hicks.

"Not our jurisdiction, remember?" he said,

shoving the door open with his shoulder. The flimsy lock busted and the door swung wide. The faint smell of decomposition lingered in the air. The cold winter air had slowed the process but that dead guy was definitely disintegrating into a pile of gunk.

We followed the adults into the house, careful not to touch anything. I covered my nose as the smell became stronger. "Why are humans so gross?" I asked mostly to myself. I inched closer for a better look. The corpse was on its back, staring up at the ceiling, a giant gash in his throat.

"Guess we know how he bit it," Dylan quipped, staring dispassionately at the dead guy that we both recognized within seconds.

I could almost feel his fucking hands on my throat, smell his rancid breath on my cheek. I swallowed, sharing a look with Dylan, confirming, "That's him. That's Asshole Darryl. Looks like Madame Moirai decided it was time to do some layoffs."

Neither of us felt anything but satisfaction that he'd died gurgling on his own blood. There was no telling how many auction girls he'd abused before meeting his end. Personally, I would've liked to see more evidence of his suffering before he bled out but dead was dead and that was enough.

"Why do you think they used a knife and not a gun?" Dylan asked, curious.

"Knife is quieter," I supposed. "Probably learned their lesson from their failed attempt at offing us. Guns going off attracts a lot of unwanted attention."

"Decent theory," Dylan said, shrugging. The fact that we were discussing methods of murder with the casual calm of going over a grocery list wasn't lost on me — or Kerri by her expression.

Hicks, on the other hand, was more interested in examining the body. I appreciated that his narrow focus didn't leave much room for worrying about our broken psyches.

I hated to play to stereotypes but sometimes they just rang true no matter how hard you tried to avoid them.

Kerri had more empathy, even if she wasn't the hugging type. I could see in her eyes that she worried what our end game looked like after this experience. We might be irrevocably broken inside. I guess that was a problem for later. I flicked my gaze away from hers and returned to watching Hicks.

Hicks bent closer, using a pen to gingerly examine the gash in his neck and the dried blood. "Hasn't been dead all that long. Maybe a day or two?" He glanced around the place. "Looks like someone was looking for something." Hicks glanced our way. "Got any idea what that might've been?"

"I don't know. Maybe anything that tied Darryl to Madame Moirai?" I guessed with a shrug. "It's not like I knew the guy. We weren't BFFs or anything."

Hicks rose and did a quick search of the small house. He returned, motioning for Kerri to follow. Of course, I wasn't going to be left behind, so I tagged along. Dylan wasn't far behind either.

Hicks went to the bedroom. It was just as trashed as the other rooms. Someone had definitely been searching for something but it was anyone's guess what or if they found what they were looking for.

However, Hicks had an eye for detail, something of a gift, I'd come to realize. He may be a drunk most days but he saw things most people didn't.

"Did you see a cat anywhere?" he asked.

"No," Kerri answered, glancing around. "Why?"

He left the room and we followed as he went to the laundry room where an old washing machine and matching dryer sat looking sad and decrepit. Hicks pointed at the big kitty litter bucket. "Because what's a guy without cats doing with a big bucket of kitty litter?"

He reached for the bucket and popped the lid. I frowned in confusion. I started, "Well, maybe he was using it for something else—" but then Hicks dumped it out and a smaller, buried container dropped to the floor. He scooped it up and opened the lid.

"Bingo," he said, smiling. "Look what I found."

We watched as he pulled a huge wad of cash, a security badge of some sort, and a fake ID that matched the name on his badge. Hicks pocketed the cash, ignoring Kerri's immediate disapproving scowl, and then handed the other materials to Kerri.

"Aren't you forgetting something?" Kerri asked, gesturing to the cash.

"Look, we both know you're not calling this in. As far as anyone knows, whoever trashed this place and killed the stiff, took whatever might be missing from this place. I call this fair compensation for a job well done," he said, grinning.

Dylan's smile said she didn't have a problem with it either. Only Kerri and I had issues with stealing from a dead guy and an active crime scene but I wasn't about to make waves for Asshole Darryl. The fucker deserved everything he got and that included losing his money.

Realizing now wasn't the time to argue ethics, she said, "All right, let's get out of here before we're seen," motioning for us to follow.

We took one final look around the place, and split. Using my burner phone, Kerri called the local police department to report the body anonymously.

"You should've left him to get eaten by wild animals," Dylan said. "He doesn't deserve a fucking burial."

"Did he hurt you?" Kerri asked.

"Everyone in that place hurt me," Dylan responded flatly and I couldn't disagree. The wounds left from that place would remain with us forever even if the physical evidence eventually faded away. "He's lucky he was already dead. I wouldn't hesitate to kill him if he weren't."

"Which is why I wanted you to stay in the car," Kerri returned with a short shake of her head. "Look, I know it's not what we were hoping for but I'm going to back to the station and run this ID as well as look into the security company on this badge. We didn't come away empty-handed."

"And I'm springing for pizza," Hicks laughed, his smoke-ravaged voice sounding like wet gravel when he ended with a cough. "Extra anchovies."

"You put fucking fish on a pizza and I'll gut you in your sleep, old man," Dylan promised. "Also, you should probably think about quitting smoking. You sound like shit."

"The devil will just have to wait his turn," Hicks said, not the least bit soured by Dylan's threat. He had a shit ton of cash in his pocket, a thick payday he hadn't expected and that was like hitting some lucky slots in Vegas. He wasn't above enjoying the moment.

Whatever, I didn't mind. I was disappointed that our trip hadn't revealed much more than a corpse but we did have more to go on than before. For the first time in a while, I felt the flutters of hope beginning to flap its wings. Maybe Kerri was right, everyone made mistakes. All we had to do was follow the trail and look for the breadcrumbs.

In the meantime, pizza was as good a way to celebrate being alive than anything else.

And I agreed with Dylan, if he dared to put anchovies on that pizza, Hicks was going to wake up dead, too.

22

A few days later Badger walked into Hicks' apartment like he owned the place, eliciting little more than an annoyed look from Hicks from his desk before he returned to his task.

Dylan glanced up from the magazine she was thumbing through as if she knew Badger was bound to show up sooner or later but I was surprised to see him.

He dropped into a chair with an expectant look in his hard eyes, an edge about him that I was beginning to understand was an indication he was in a mood.

"What's a paying customer gotta do around here to get a fucking update?" he said.

I could only imagine how it must gall a man like

Hicks to have Badger dragging him around by his nut sac but we all had our crosses to hear, right?

Hicks ignored him, a dangerous decision by my book and I filled the tense silence with my own update. "We haven't found anything on Nova," I said, "but the one of the guards that Madame Moirai hired was found dead in his house upstate."

"Yeah? How'd the fucker die?" Badger asked, mildly interested. "Broken fingers, toes and other dangly bits before they put a plugged his grey matter?"

"Nope. Slit his throat," Dylan answered, bored. "Looks like he died relatively quick and easy. Too good for him, if you ask me."

"Ahh, that's the problem with modern-day killers, no fucking imagination. That's a pity," he said, returning quickly to his first query. "Time's ticking Hicks. What you got for me?"

Hicks growled, "The girls already told you. We're slim on leads but we've got a few we're still chasing down. You coming here and pestering me with your bullshit isn't going to produce results any faster."

"That doesn't work for me," Badger said with a darkening scowl. "I put money in your hand to give me answers, not excuses. I've already lost my best runner and now you're telling me I don't even get answers about my sister. Makes me fucking grumpy, old man."

"Yeah, well we all got problems," Hicks returned, unimpressed. "Go ruin someone else's day. I'm fucking busy."

"Cut the shit, Badger," Dylan said, tossing the magazine. "If you've got a job for me to do, just spit it out. You don't have to pretend that you're all jacked up about our situation. We all know your ability to care about anyone beyond yourself is limited."

"I'm fucking crushed," Badger said flatly, narrowing his gaze at Dylan as if deciding whether or not he wanted to pop her in the mouth. I'd never seen Badger hit Dylan but I had no doubt he wouldn't hesitate if the mood struck him. Not that Dylan couldn't take care of herself but I couldn't promise that I wouldn't jump on his back like a vampiric spider monkey if he tried.

But the tension ebbed as Badger shrugged, Dylan's analysis bouncing off his shoulders. "Maybe. But I am down a runner and seeing as I've paid for something and gotten nothing...I'm gonna need a little better customer service."

I stared with disgust. "Are you demanding sexual favors?" I asked hotly.

Dylan answered first with a snort. "I'd bite his fucking dick off and he knows it."

Badger smirked at her threat. "As tempting the offer is, you're like my sister and the thought makes me want to vomit. I do have standards."

I caught the subtle hurt in Dylan's expression but it was gone in a blink as she reminded him sourly, "I never said I wasn't willing to run. I need to get out of this place anyway before I go insane."

Damn it, Dylan. I saw very clearly what Badger could not. She was willing to put herself in danger just to show Badger that she was still his No. 1. "We need to stay put," I said, trying to talk some sense into her. "Besides, Kerri's going to be back soon enough after she's had a chance to run down that Baker chick."

"What Baker chick?" Badger asked.

Hicks answered, cutting me off. "Might be a lead, might be a dead end. I'll tell you if anything pops up about Nova. That was the deal."

Badger grunted. "Yeah, okay." He looked to me. "You doing okay?"

"I'm fine."

I felt rather than saw the flare of jealousy in Dylan's eyes and I didn't want to have anything to do with it. I wasn't into Badger and I wasn't about to pay the price for Dylan thinking I was. I rose and excused myself, ready to end my part in this little drama. "I'm taking a nap. Let me know if Kerri shows up. Otherwise, don't bother me unless this place is on fire."

And I left them behind, closing the bedroom door with a firm click. I wanted to tell Dylan she could do better than a sociopathic Gen Z crime lord but how did I know that for sure? What kind of future did we have when this was all over? The life I had seemed a distant memory, belonging to someone else.

I remembered walking the halls of my high school, complaining about the things most kids bitched about — homework, dick teachers, and guys that left us on 'read' — but that seemed like another life now.

It was the reason Lora couldn't understand why I wouldn't just 'let her dad handle this' as she put it because kids weren't supposed to have to deal with shit like this.

I've seen more dead bodies in the last month than most people see in their average lifetime.

I couldn't see myself going to college, pretending as if none of this had happened to me, moving on to sit in a class and listen to some professor drone on about shit that really had no meaning when girls were being snatched out of thin air and buried without anyone taking notice.

I thought of Henri and how smugly he'd believed that my life didn't matter because I was just an object, a thing to be used and abused because he paid for the privilege but *his* kids were worth far more.

He wouldn't dream of putting his kids on the block, now would he?

I rolled to my side to stare out of the bedroom window. The light sound of rain hitting the pane was soothing but plucked at a sadness that I couldn't quite escape.

There would always be this hole punched inside me, one that I would never be able to patch and I didn't know how to escape the inevitable consequences. I wasn't stupid. Emotional wounds created the most baggage that eventually became unbearable to carry. My mother was an alcoholic for a reason. Not that I was brimming with sympathy for that toxic hag — particularly after her latest media stunt — but I knew that people didn't spring from the dirt with issues. As impossible as it seemed, Carla West had been born with a clean slate, innocent and unsullied by life. I loved my Gran but I could tell she probably wasn't always the best to have around. She was different by the time I came around but there's no telling what kind of scars she left behind on her only daughter.

I didn't want to think about the past. The past was dead. If I didn't get my present figured out, my future would be dead, too.

Why had Madame Moirai had Asshole Darryl killed? Was it really just cleaning up loose ends? Or was he paying for his screw-up that night when I blew everything to shit?

I hoped I was the reason.

I shuddered and hugged the pillow. If Madame Moirai was paying my mom to play the concerned parent she didn't do her homework because I would never come running at the sight of my mom crying big ol' crocodile tears. My mom would never cry for me. She'd spent my entire life never missing an opportunity to tell me how I'd ruined her life so why the hell would I believe that she actually cared if I was gone?

Fuck her.

The tears stinging my eyes felt like a betrayal by my own body. Okay, so no matter how wretched your parents are...you still wanted them to care, somewhere, deep down.

I guess I was like everybody else.

Being alone was a terrible feeling. Feeling alone while being hunted was terrifying.

I sniffed back my worthless tears just in time to hear the front door open and shut. I climbed from the bed and peered into the living room. Dylan and Badger were gone. I frowned with disappointment. I looked to Hicks with accusation in my eyes to ask, "You let her go with him?"

"Not sure I could really stop her," he said, grabbing a pack of cigarettes only to find it empty. He tossed it away with annoyance, searching his desk for a different pack until I went to stand in front of his desk, arms folded. "What?" he asked, still disgruntled.

"You know she's doing illegal shit when she's running with Badger," I said. "How can you, as a former cop, just let her do that?"

"Because kid, I ain't no cop no more, remember?"

"Yeah, I can see why," I grumbled. "Seriously, Hicks...she's just a kid."

He sighed and leaned back in his chair, his back popping with the effort. "The way I see it, that girl ain't been a kid for a long time. She's got the heart of a stone-cold killer. Remember that."

"No, you don't know her," I said. "It's easy to judge someone based on so little. You see a girl with a rough past and sketchy background and you automatically assume that's all she is."

"Yeah? So you tell me who she really is, then," he challenged, finally finding a pack with cigarettes. He made a grand, flourishing gesture, before lighting up, "Enlighten me."

I should've just told him to fuck off and returned to the room but I needed to stick up for Dylan, maybe so I could reassure myself that I wasn't wrong about her. "She's fierce and loyal. She'll put herself in harm's way if it means protecting someone she loves. She's been through more than most but she's not a terrible person."

"You're pretty defensive of a girl who regularly tells you to shut the fuck up," he pointed out with wry amusement. "You're more forgiving than most."

"She doesn't mean anything by it," I said. "I mean, it's rude and whatever but she sticks up for me when it counts."

That much was true. Dylan was a rough one, hard around the edges and often spit acid but I knew she'd beat someone to death or die trying if anyone threatened me.

How did I know? Because I would do the same for her.

I rubbed at my nose. "Have you found anything

on Tana's grandmother?" I asked, needing to think about something else.

Hicks' expression said it all. *Of course not.* "Look, like Kerri said, it's tough enough to find a needle in a haystack when you know what you're looking for but when you're feeling around blind? Shit, that's damn near impossible. That fight is one you're going to have to let go. We got bigger problems. Besides, didn't you say the grandma's got dementia or something?"

"Yeah," I said morosely. "But that makes it worse. She doesn't understand why Tana is gone...just that someone who cared for her never came home. I don't know, it just eats at me. Tana loved her grandmother more than herself. Madame Moirai took advantage of that love and killed Tana with it."

Hicks' expression softened. "I know, kid. I promise you, we're going to do whatever it takes to bring that bitch and her entire fucking network down, okay?"

I believed him. He was a drunk and a morally ambiguous gun for hire but I saw the truth in his eyes. Maybe he worried that his daughter might someday get caught in Madame Moirai's crosshairs or maybe he was genuinely bit by the justice bug but he wasn't going to rest until he had answers and that gave me a much-needed sliver of hope.

I nodded, accepting his promise.

"I'm hungry, I announced, breaking the heavy silence. "Chinese take-out?"

"You make the order, I'll pay the bill."

I grinned. Maybe it wasn't so bad stealing from a really bad dead guy.

I couldn't do anything about Dylan running off with Badger except hope that she doesn't get her stupid ass killed and I couldn't find Tana's grandmother without more details but I could eat my feelings with the help of Mr. Wong's China House.

So, bring on the mu-shu pork.

23

Sometimes you can't play by the rules.

Hicks and Kerri were bound by the law, mostly, but all bets were off as far as Dylan and I were concerned.

A few days later, Hicks went out to get food and cigarettes, and I took the opportunity to snoop around his desk. I knew he was hiding something, probably on the guise of protecting us but I wasn't looking for a guardian angel. We wanted movement and answers.

Within a few minutes of searching, I held up a small slip of paper scribbled with barely legible penmanship. I showed it to Dylan. "Want to go on a field trip?"

"To where?" she asked.

"Regina Baker's place."

She narrowed her gaze with a bloodthirsty grin. "Hell yeah."

I returned the smile. "You think you can talk Badger into going with us to provide the scare factor? Even with the element of surprise, we're going to need some muscle and possibly some firepower."

"I think that's doable. Badger's been itching for payback. This might scratch that itch for a little bit. What about Hicks and the cop?"

I couldn't think about that right now. "Some things you just have to handle on your own. Kerri is trying to build a case. I'm not. The way I figure it, if they all end up in the ground, that's better justice than anything the District Attorney can dish out."

Dylan didn't argue. "I like your savage side," she said. "I was beginning to wonder if you'd lost it somewhere along the way."

"Not lost, just biding my time." I shoved the address into my back pocket and swung my jacket over my shoulders. "Let's go. Hicks is bound to show up soon and I don't want him to stop us from doing what needs to be done."

Dylan nodded, grabbed her own jacket and we were out of there like the devil was tracking our steps. On the way, Dylan called Badger, gave him the address and told him to meet us there.

It was dark and wet outside. New York in the winter wasn't all winter wonderland and picturesque postcards. It was a lot like New York in the summer except instead of sweltering with humidity, the streets were covered in dirty slush and it was colder than a witch's tit. Also, the smell of the city never quite went away. Knowing what I knew now, I wondered if it was simply the rotten core of humanity leaching through to the atmosphere. *Take a whiff of that corruption, ain't it great?*

The apartment building wasn't far. We climbed the fire escape like monkeys, the rust coating the wet metal biting into my skin. The light drizzle quickly dampened our clothes but we climbed with single-minded focus. True to her claim, Badger was eager to play our dangerous game if it meant fucking up someone who had anything to do with Nova's death.

There was no doubt Badger was a bad guy but his love for Nova had been real. Just like Dylan's.

I was climbing that fire escape for Tana, Jilly and myself. I hungered for answers, but also for blood.

Badger lead the way. He stopped with the stealth of a ninja, signaling for us to wait as he jimmied the window lock open. The window slid up with a slight whine and we dropped inside the apartment on noiseless feet. My heart hammered in my chest, reminding me of the night we escaped the auction house.

Regina Baker, the only person we'd been able to identify from the auction house that wasn't dead at this point, was going to give us answers if we had to pop every finger from the knuckle. Dylan was right, a savage did live inside me and Regina was going to regret awakening that beast.

But in an instant, everything changed with deadly speed.

Something swung and knocked Badger upside the head with a sickening crack. He dropped like a stone. I didn't have time to do anything but react. I dove for the floor, tucking and rolling in the darkness, hoping to avoid whoever had known we were coming and started swinging like a fucking Major Leaguer.

Glass shattered and Dylan grunted. My eyes adjusted quickly to the dark and I saw the square build of Regina Baker. I kicked out with brutal rage, connecting with her knee. I watched her buckle with a scream as the knee went in the opposite direction. I rolled away from her and scrambled to my feet, searching for a light. My fumbling fingers found a light switch and I flipped it, flooding the apartment with light. Badger was face-down on the carpet, not moving and Dylan was holding her shoulder, her lips compressed in a tight grimace of quiet pain but it was Regina who was making a ridiculous racket, howling like a fucking banshee as she held her shattered kneecap. I ripped the cell phone charger wire free from the wall and tied Regina up while she writhed, then stuffed a dirty sock deep in her mouth to shut her squalling.

On her way to check Badger, Dylan wound up and kicked Regina square in her thick gut. "You fucking bitch," she muttered. "Shoe's on the other foot now, isn't it?"

She kneeled by Badger and gently rolled him over. He had a nasty crack and it was bleeding like a motherfucker. I quickly found a towel and Dylan pressed it to his head. "Head wounds bleed bad but I think he's going to be okay," Dylan said as she not-so-gently tapped his cheek to wake him up. "C'mon fucker, you have work to do. No sleeping on the job."

Badger's eyes opened, two round orbs bouncing around in his skull like loose marbles for a second until his vision cleared and he struggled to sit up. "What the fuck...?" he grumbled, closing his eyes again as he got his bearing.

"She got the jump on us," Dylan answered. "The

bitch must have supersonic hearing because she was waiting for us the minute we cleared the window."

I gestured to the thick block of a woman still on the floor, breathing hard against the pain. Dylan and I dragged Regina to a chair and tossed her into it. Badger rose unsteadily to his feet but I could tell he was regaining his focus and I didn't feel bad for whatever Badger was going to dish out to the ugly cunt staring daggers at us.

Badger tossed the bloody towel even though his head wound continued to dribble. He leaned into Regina's space with a menacing growl. "You fucking cracked my dome, bitch. That's not very neighborly of you."

She made ugly gagging noises as she tried to talk around the nasty ass sock stuffed in her mouth. Badger reached in and popped the sock free. Regina took a deep breath and immediately started screaming her head off but Badger was prepared this time and punched her hard. Blood gushed from her broken nose as it dribbled snotty red slime. He wagged his finger at her as she gulped her own gack, shuddering. "Do it again and I'll bust your teeth out, you hear me? Are we understanding each other?" he asked in a silky tone that was creepy as fuck.

Regina jerked a short nod, remaining quiet even as she was probably in excruciating pain.

"That's better," Badger said, caressing her jaw. "See? We can be civil. It doesn't have to be so nasty, does it?" He didn't wait for her answer, adding ruefully, "Well, I mean, it *will* probably get nasty because you fucking cracked my skull open and I don't suffer that kind of disrespect but that can wait a little bit. Maybe if you answer all my questions, I'll feel more generous than I'm feeling right now. You feeling me? Yeah, I think you do."

"I don't fucking know you," she said, her voice garbled but her gaze darted to me and Dylan and she knew exactly who we were even if Badger was a mystery. "You broke into my house and I was defending myself."

"Bullshit," I spat. "How'd you know we were coming?"

Her gaze narrowed. "I didn't know you were coming. I thought you might be someone else."

I narrowed my stare. "What do you mean?" The memory flashed of Asshole Darryl lying dead in his living room and I realized Madame Moirai might be doing a massive house cleaning, from top to bottom. "You thought Madame Moirai had sent someone to kill you," I surmised, folding my arms across my chest. "Can't say you don't deserve it but why's she trying to kill you? You were one of her crew."

"You ruined everything," Regina spat, spearing me with a look of hatred so intense it almost had form. "You fucked us all with your stupid escape."

Rage curdled my insides and threatened to incinerate everything in its path. "Fuck you, I'm a victim and you're a fucking predator," I seethed, amazed that she saw herself as anything but a rotten person from the inside out. "How fucking dare you blame me for shit! Did you ever think of how many lives you were ruining with your little scheme? We were fucking kids, you psychopath!"

Dylan held me back, eyeing Regina. "So...what's the deal? Madame Moirai is closing up shop and permanently retiring the employees?"

"Something like that," she answered, her face pale from the pain. She shifted her gaze back to me with accusation. "You broke my fucking knee, you little cunt."

I faked a sweet smile. "Well, I guess today's my lucky day. Maybe I ought to play the Lottery, too."

"I'm done with story hour," Dylan muttered, grabbing Regina by the shirt drawing her close enough to smell her corrupt soul. "Listen up, you filthy fucking pedophile, we know all about your previous record for messing around with kids and that you only spent a fraction of time in prison when you should've rotted and died behind bars. Who the fuck is Madame Moirai that she can pull those kinds of strings?"

Regina's mouth stretched in an ugly, blood-stained smile. "You think I'm stupid enough to tell you shit? *Fuck you.* You were never supposed to leave that house. You're living on borrowed time so enjoy it. Once The Avalon has your number, you can never outrun their reach."

"Who the fuck are The Avalon?" Dylan growled, shaking Regina hard. "If you don't fucking start talking, I'm going to let my friend bleed you dry, drop by drop until you're nothing but a fucking dried up husk for the cops to find just like your friend, Asshole Darryl." Her gaze widened as if she hadn't known he was dead. Dylan grinned and shoved Regina out of her grasp. "Yeah, that fucker is dead, too. Who else is dead? You must've known that a massive house cleaning was happening otherwise you wouldn't have been waiting for someone to sneak into your place in the middle of the night."

"And why should I tell you?" Regina asked, breathing hard against the pain. "I got no loyalty to the merch."

"The merch?" I repeated, a hot flush washing over me. "We are fucking human beings, you toxic cunt."

"No, you're the property of The Avalon and they never let go of property they've purchased," Regina returned with a cold stare. "And they've got connections you can't even fathom. You're all going to die."

"What if we offered you protection from Madame Moirai...would you help us?" I asked, swallowing my hatred.

"Ain't no one safe from her and The Avalon, don't you get it? They're fucking *global*. There's nowhere you can run, nowhere you can hide. Eventually, she'll find you and put you where you were always destined to be — in the ground."

Fear prickled my skin. "Tell us who she is. Give us a fighting fucking chance," I said. "For once, do something good in your life. Help us!"

But Regina wasn't going to help. She wanted to see us suffer. I should've known she got off on the idea of our fear.

"I hope you die screaming," Regina said, her mouth twisting with cruelty. My heart stuttered a beat at the pure wickedness in her stare. She wasn't sorry for anything she'd done and she wanted to inflict as much pain as possible before dying.

My voice shook as I promised, "You're going to die here."

Undeterred, Regina leaned forward, straining against the ties binding her to the chair, focusing on me. "Did he rip you open when he fucked your ass? Did you like it? Your buyer must've really been into you...he rarely puts in a bid for elevation...except for you...you were different. You should've taken the deal."

Henri's hateful face popped into my memory and I started to shake, my vision blurring.

Badger stepped forward and pushed me and Dylan aside, his eyes hard as flint. Playtime was over. I didn't feel bad for Regina. She deserved to suffer but the malicious energy radiating from Badger's gaze told me things were about to get real messy...and super painful.

He got real close and personal into Regina's face. "Here's the thing, love...under ordinary circumstances, I stay out of other people's playgrounds but your little operation killed my sister...and she was the only thing keeping that tiny spark of humanity alive inside me. Now that she's gone...I feel next to nothing for nobody. Almost like...my soul was snuffed out, you feeling me? So, your time's up and

I'm done with your bullshit if you ain't got nothing worth listening to."

Before she could babble a response, I handed him the sock and he stuffed it hard back into her mouth. Her eyes bugged with fear as he pulled a long switchblade from his back pocket.

I felt Dylan's hand slip into mine and squeeze in silent solidarity.

And then, I watched with cold dispassion as he proceeded to carve Regina Baker like a Christmas turkey.

Some people deserved exactly what they got — and sometimes, you were lucky enough to witness karma in all its gory glory at work.

24

The following day, Kerri burst into the apartment, eyes blazing as she said, "Regina Baker is fucking dead. Anyone in this rat-infested apartment know anything about that?"

Hicks swore under his breath as he narrowed his gaze at me and Dylan, knowing in that instant exactly what Kerri suspected. "You little shits couldn't stay put for two fucking seconds, could you?"

"You don't know what they did to us," Dylan returned coldly, not bothering to deny anything. "You've got no room to judge."

"Did you kill her?" Kerri asked.

"I did not," Dylan answered with fake innocence.

"Neither did I," I volunteered with the same tone.

Not a lie. Badger killed her. We simply did nothing to save her...just as she'd done nothing to save us.

A fucked up eye-for-an-eye scenario but appropriate, if you asked me.

"Well, good job girls, you may have just fucked our only goddamn lead," Kerri spat, dropping onto the lumpy sofa as if she'd just crumpled beneath the weight of our situation. "I can't fucking help you if you keep going behind my back and making things harder for me to make any headway."

I felt a smidge of guilt for Kerri but I wasn't capable of feeling guilty for what'd happened to Regina. The world was better off without her.

"Do they know who killed Regina?" I asked.

"No leads," Kerri answered pointedly, which told me she must've removed anything that might've pointed in our direction. It wasn't fair of us to expect Kerri to put her career on the line for us but we were already walking this path and we couldn't double-back, which is probably what Kerri recognized, too. *In for a penny, in for a pound* as Gran would say. Kerri added gruffly, "The woman had plenty of enemies. No telling who cut her to pieces but I do know...whoever did it, is a fucking psychopath."

"More like a sociopath," I murmured in disagreement, then shrugged, adding, "but who knows? Like you said, the woman had enemies."

Hicks was annoyed as fuck because he figured out we'd swiped the address from his desk, saying tersely, "Let's cut the shit, what'd you learn?"

"Nothing," I answered morosely. "She didn't tell us anything. Just that The Avalon was never going to let us go, and that after our escape Madame Moirai started cleaning house. Regina was expecting someone to put a bullet in her brain but she wasn't going to go down without a fight."

"You hurt?" Kerri asked.

I shook my head, declining to mention that Badger had a nasty concussion and Dylan had a vicious bruise on her arm from taking a whack from the steel pipe Regina had been wielding. Honestly, I was shocked that Regina hadn't broken Dylan's arm and killed Badger but as I was starting to realize, they were fucking hard to kill.

Point in our favor.

"Damn it," Kerri grumbled, still fuming but she needed to keep moving. "I got something to share."

That perked us up. "Yeah? What?"

"Look, what I'm about to tell you isn't great but it proves the hunch that whoever the fuck this Madame Moirai and her network is, it's pretty damn connected."

"Yeah, fucking *global*, as Regina put it," Dylan said.

"Well, she wasn't lying, which makes our odds pretty bleak."

I shrugged, refusing to let the fear souring my gut show in my expression. "Yeah, so? It's not like we thought we had good odds going into this. What did you find out?"

"When I was doing a missing person search within specific perimeters, I found a disturbing pattern...one that was missed before. Seven missing girls fit the criteria. All seven were later identified in the morgue through police records, including...a girl named Nova Kasey."

Dylan stilled, her face paling. "You found Nova?"

Kerri nodded. "The official cause of death was listed as a drug overdose."

"Bullshit. Nova didn't do drugs," Dylan said, her voice strangled. "They fucking lied."

"Are you sure? Maybe you didn't know Nova as well as you think you did," Kerri said, trying to be gentle but Dylan wasn't having it.

"Fuck you, Kerri. Don't pull that shit with me. I'm telling you right now, Nova didn't do fucking drugs. The girl wouldn't even touch alcohol. If they found drugs in her system, they put them there."

Dylan's eyes were dry but I felt her anguish. "If she was found and autopsied...that means she's buried somewhere, right?" I asked.

"Yeah, the city contracts with several private mortuaries for unclaimed bodies. They pay a reduced amount for each body and the deceased are afforded some modicum of dignity. Nova was buried by Lawson & Bergstein Mortuary, according to the file."

"She has a grave somewhere?" Dylan asked, blinking rapidly. "You mean, like someplace we could visit her?"

"Technically, yeah — assuming the information is accurate. Sometimes people get sloppy when there isn't outside accountability."

"What does that mean?" I asked.

"It means that if no one is gonna ask about a dead drug addict, then, sometimes details get lost or mixed up," Hicks answered, shaking his head. "I've seen it happen back when I was on the force. I was chasing down a lead on a dead prostitute, kinda similar story. The original cause of death was listed as an accidental overdose but I found new evidence that suggested she was murdered. I tried to have the body exhumed but the body wasn't where it was supposed to be. Turns out the person responsible for typing up the report wasn't paying attention to details and ended up losing the burial information and just guessed, figuring no one was going to follow up."

"That's fucked up," I said, disturbed by how little others cared about people. "What happened?"

"Nothing. The case went cold again. We couldn't narrow down where her body might've ended up. My superior told me to wrap it up and let it go. I didn't have a choice but to do as I was told. We were understaffed and overworked as it was...no one had my back when I tried pushing against orders."

"Because no one cares about dead prostitutes, right?" Dylan guessed with a hard look. "Good enough to fuck but not good enough to care if they die?"

"Sorry kid, I wish the truth wasn't so shitty," Hicks said.

We were lumped up into that category. Good

enough to spend a shit-ton of money on for that first dip but then, thrown away like trash when they were done.

"I want to see where she's buried," Dylan said, wiping at her eyes.

But Hicks shook his head. "That's a bad idea," he warned. "That's like laying cheese for the mouse. You can't go where they'll expect you to turn up."

If I couldn't turn up at my house or Lora's, Dylan couldn't mourn her beloved Nova either. I gave her a look that told her I understood even as I agreed with Hicks, promising, "When this is all over, we'll go together. For now, you need to steer clear. For all we know, they could be watching and waiting for you."

"I don't care," Dylan said bitterly. "I need to know where she's buried."

But Kerri wasn't finished. "That's not all. When I pulled Nova's file, someone noticed, which means someone in my department has reason to care. My superior came in and told me to stop wasting time on a closed case."

"Closed case? How the fuck can they close the case when she was murdered?" Dylan asked.

"Not according to her autopsy and that's what the official record states," Kerri explained.

"This is some bullshit," Dylan said, her voice

rising an octave. "If some rich girl had ended up like Nova, that shit would've been sprayed all over the news with cops tripping all over themselves to solve the crime. It's not Nova's fault that she had shitty parents. It's not any of our faults!"

Kerri waited a beat for Dylan to calm down. It wasn't that Dylan wasn't spitting truth, it was only that there was nothing Kerri could do about it. When she sensed Dylan was finished, she continued, "There were other discrepancies in her autopsy that looked like red flags to me."

"Like what?" I asked.

"She had bruising that I feel is more consistent with what you girls described than what was written in the report. The girl was beaten."

"So who the fuck wrote this bogus report?" Dylan demanded to know. "Maybe we ought to start there. He or she is obviously crooked as fuck. They must be working for Madame Moirai."

"I thought the same thing. I looked into the coroner who processed Nova's body..."

"And?" Hicks asked.

"Dead. Heart attack about six weeks ago."

"Jesus fucking Christ," Hicks muttered. "Working for this bitch seems like a death sentence no matter where you are in the chain."

"Maybe. Or he might've died from natural causes. Apparently, he was pretty old and getting ready to retire."

"I don't understand...if Nova was found... wouldn't they have contacted her next of kin?" I asked.

"Under normal circumstances but I checked her file and the only contact information was an old foster home and there were no other numbers listed. When the city can't find next of kin, they process the deceased as indigent."

"What the fuck does that mean?" Dylan asked, offended.

"It just means she was poor and unable to pay for burial expenses," I answered, soothing Dylan's feelings. I looked at Kerri. "So, basically, we have a dead coroner, a murdered girl, some random mortuary and Madame Moirai going on a killing spree trying to cut loose ties. That sound about right?"

"Pretty accurate thus far." She looked to Hicks. "You want to add anything?"

"Yeah," he said, reaching for the whiskey bottle "I'm going to need a helluva lot more of this if I'm going to get through this shit-show with my sanity. This whole goddamn mess is like something out of a fucking movie and I'm definitely not getting paid enough."

"Glad to know you're only it for the money," Dylan retorted. "I hope you get cirrhosis."

"I'm sure that cosmic order is already in process, kid," Hicks returned, not the least bit ruffled.

"Enough, you two," Kerri sighed, rubbing her brow. "Look, I understand why you girls did what you did...but you can't go vigilante on me, okay? Regina Baker was a shit person but she was our *one* solid lead. I might've been able to get her to talk."

"Not to burst your bubble but she wasn't going to say shit," Dylan said. "Especially not to some cop. She deserved what she got and I don't regret a thing." With that, Dylan abruptly rose and left the room, slamming the bedroom door behind her.

Even though Dylan had claimed that she preferred to believe that Nova was dead because it hurt less...the reality was different.

Removing all doubt that Nova was gone, had to hurt like a hole in the chest.

Adding to her burden, Dylan would have to give the news to Badger.

I shared a look with Hicks and he knew what I was thinking.

"I'll tell him. It's what he's paying me for anyway," he said, pursing his lips before lifting the bottle and taking a deep swig. "Fuck, this job is going to kill me one way or another any way. Who wants to live forever, right?"

Hicks rose and grabbed his jacket. To Kerri, he instructed, "Keep them here, will ya? I'm going to deliver the news and I don't need either of these little idiots stirring up more trouble while I'm gone."

I was touched by his odd show of concern. Kerri nodded and watched him leave.

To me, she said, "Have you eaten?"

I shrugged. I wasn't really hungry. I was worried about Dylan. Kerri sighed and went to the kitchen to survey what was available. Hicks wasn't so good about stocking the cupboard, a fact Kerri discovered within a few minutes of searching. "That man," she muttered, mostly to herself. "Okay, looks like take-out. What sounds good?"

"I don't care," I said, still thinking about Nova and how she'd suffered the same fate as a lot of auction girls, like Tana. Maybe they'd had the same buyer. "Why do they get off on hurting people?" I asked.

Kerri paused, unsure of how to answer. Finally,

she just shook her head. "I don't know, kid. Some people are just fucking evil, I guess."

The truth wasn't much comfort.

In fact, the truth scared the ever-loving shit out of me.

25

"C'mon, we're going on another field trip," Hicks announced, abruptly rousing both of us from our bed. "This train is leaving in five. Let's go."

"Go without me," Dylan mumbled, burrowing more deeply into the blankets. She hadn't left the bed in days since discovering Nova was dead. It was like all the fight had just leached out through the puncture hole of her grief. Nothing seemed to help. I stopped trying to get her up and simply laid next to her, holding her hand.

I didn't realize how quickly a broken heart could derail even the most steadfast of vengeance trains until I saw Dylan withdraw into herself. Say what you would about Dylan but she loved with the ferocity of a guard dog. Nova had been her touchstone, just as she'd been for Badger.

Now, both were unmoored.

For Badger, it meant he was roaming the city a loose cannon, dangerous and unpredictable. I was glad he wasn't around. I didn't have the mental bandwidth to tap dance around his moods. With my luck, I'd say the wrong thing and end up in that goddamn pit of his, which I wanted to avoid.

But for Dylan, she was curling inward like a dying flower and I didn't know how to help her.

I moved closer to whisper, "You have to get out of this bed at some point. We can't let *her* win otherwise, all the girls lost to Madame Moirai's auction will never see justice. We're the only ones speaking for them. Tana, Jilly...Nova...they need us to be stronger than we've ever been before. You and me, girl, we got this. C'mon, don't quit on me now."

"What does it matter? She's gone. They're all gone. It's just a matter of time before we are, too. We can't win this game, Nicole. Don't you get it? We're fucked."

"With that attitude, yeah," I said. "But you're stronger than this. Nova is watching you. Are you going to just lay down and die? Is that what she would've wanted for you?"

"Fuck you," Dylan said, a tiny spark of her former self showing itself with an angry spark, which was exactly what I wanted to see. "You can't rally the situation into something it's not. We're fucking outgunned. She wins. End of story. I'm tired of fighting it. If you had any fucking brains, you'd admit it, too."

I realized there was only one way to handle Dylan and I'd gone about it all wrong. I rolled away from Dylan to stand, yanking the bedding from her curled body. "No," I said firmly. "You don't get to check out, you selfish little bitch. I didn't risk my fucking neck to save your ass just so you could quit when I need you the most. Yeah, Nova is gone...so are a lot of fucking girls and it's our job to do what they couldn't — survive long enough to break Madame Moirai and her fucking network of perverted dickheads."

Dylan sat up, her eyes hot as she tried to wrench the bedding back. "Yeah? Who says?"

"I do," I answered without flinching.

We held each other's stare as we each held a corner of the blanket in a mental and physical tug-of-war. I wasn't backing down. Dylan didn't respect weakness and she wasn't going to get any from me, which meant I wasn't going to let her go soft either.

"You don't understand —"

"Excuses are like assholes, everyone's got one. You're going to get up, get dressed and walk out that front door with me and then you're going to remember why the fuck we have to do this."

"And why's that?"

"Because it fucking matters. It matters to more than just you and I. If we don't stop Madame Moirai, she won't quit. More girls will die for the simple crime of hoping for a better life. I know you don't want that. I know that you wanted better, just like Nova. Just like Tana, and Jilly...like me." I held my hand to her. "So get the fuck out of that bed and come with me. We'll do this together. I swear to you, I won't rest until they've all paid the debt they owe to all of us." I inhaled a long breath and ended with a sincere, "I need you, Dylan. I can't do it without you."

Something clicked and turned over in Dylan's mind. We were sisters in a fucked up sorority and with that bond came loyalty in all its ugly glory. She climbed from the bed with a terse, "Fine" and started to dress. My shoulders lost their tension and I almost started crying from the relief. I wasn't lying. I couldn't do this without her and the thought of facing my fate alone sent tendrils of diarrhea-inducing fear to curl around my gut.

But she just showed me I wouldn't be alone.

Dressed, she stalked past me without another word but that's okay, I didn't need it. She was back on track and that's all that mattered.

Once we were in Kerri's vehicle, I discovered we were heading back to Esterdell. Hicks had found a possible location for the auction house and we were headed to check it out.

This time my gut didn't cramp as hard at the familiar landscape but as we drove closer, I started to tremble. This time it was Dylan who reached for me, squeezing hard for a brief second. I nodded, feeling the subtle shake in her own hand.

It was like facing down your attacker in a police line-up. The cops tell you you're safe and they can't see you but when only a sheet of mirrored glass stood between you and the person who nearly killed you... the glass isn't enough to quell the fear.

"I did a title search for all the houses listed within Esterdell and unlike most of the houses owned by private individuals, one was listed as owned by a corporate entity...Avalon Incorporated. Didn't seem like a fucking coincidence. Figured we might as well check it out."

A shiver raced my spine. "That has to be the auction house," I agreed, sharing a look with Dylan. We were going back to the auction house. "What if someone is still there?" I asked.

Kerri answered, "I doubt there will be. That engineer told me that the house was a complete loss. It's not safe for anyone to be in the structure at this point and it's not like that bitch is going to want more undue attention."

That made sense. I breathed a quiet sigh of relief. "You brought your gun, though, right?" I asked.

"I never leave the house without it," she assured me. "But to be on the safe side, please promise me you'll stay in the car until we give you the all-clear."

I nodded. I supposed it was the least we could do seeing as we'd killed her only good lead up until this point.

Kerri double-checked the GPS and we branched off the main road to a nicely maintained private road flanked by trees and manicured spaces. The beauty was lost on me and Dylan. The last time we'd run across these grounds we'd been fleeing for our lives.

Snow still covered the ground. My toes tingled, remembering cold feet as we ran with only stupid house slippers to protect us from frostbite.

I remembered the cold chill biting into our skin

as it penetrated our thin pajamas. I remembered the wild, panicked beat of my heart as it threatened to pop from my chest at the fear of being caught.

I also remembered vowing never to return to this awful place.

But here we were…

Kerri rolled up slowly to the massive mansion. Burnt and scorched sections of the house marred the icy beauty as wooden bones spindled into the frosty air like outstretched fingers clawing at the heavens.

After a quick look around the property, Hicks and Kerri allowed us to exit the vehicle. When Mr. Personality had picked me up and dropped me off, depositing me into the hands of that wretched little bitch Olivia, I'd had no idea how my life was going to be ruined.

How naive I must've seemed when I'd thought I was so street-smart.

I could only imagine how they'd laughed at our expense.

The faint scent of charred wood and blackened brick teased my nose. I smiled. I did this.

Kerri's breath plumed in front of her as she surveyed the house. "You did a great job of destroying this place. How'd you get the fire to spread so fast and far?"

"I placed the accelerant in all the rooms in the basement I could. I didn't want to take the chance that they'd be able to put the fire out quickly. Do you think it's safe enough to go inside?"

"It's risky," Kerri admitted. "Why do you want to go inside?"

"I don't know. I want to see the damage, I guess."

"That's a bad idea," Hicks disagreed with a frown. "The subfloor is fucked. The whole place is unstable. One wrong step and you'd go crashing through the floor."

I understood the risk. I wanted to go anyway. "If I was going to die in that house, I would've already," I said, carefully pushing open the front door. I stepped over the threshold and into the foyer. Milky sunlight pierced through giant holes in the ceiling where the fire had climbed the walls and eaten the roof. The place groaned as if the pain of the blaze was still burning through its timbers. My gaze traveled up. The stairway to the upper levels looked sturdy but as I started to climb, Hicks' hand on my arm stopped me.

"You're not going up there," he said with a firm shake of his head. I thought of shaking his hand away and going anyway but I decided I didn't need to see the room where they'd imprisoned each of us. The memory of those rooms was forever carved into my brain.

Kerri peered down the darkened stairway that lead to the basement. "This is where the morgue was?"

"And the auction," I said.

"There's likely nothing left after the fire," she mused with a frown.

Then I realized something. I whirled around to ask Dylan. "Notice anything?"

Dylan glanced around, hugging herself as if she couldn't quite shake the chill in her soul. She was about to say no but then she saw what I saw. "Everything is gone. This place is empty."

"Exactly. They came in and cleaned out everything that'd once been in this house, whether it was torched or not. They didn't want to leave behind a single trace anyone had ever lived or spent time in this house," I said. "They're covering their tracks."

"Seeing as this house is owned by a corporate entity, it's likely they furnished the house using leased furniture. I've heard of high-end clients renting fancy furniture from designers when they're trying to sell a place. It's called 'dressing' a house. Whoever they leased the furniture from would've filed an insurance report for the damaged property. We might be able to trace it and see where it leads."

"I doubt Madame Moirai is stupid enough to leave a paper trail of any kind," I said, glancing around. "She's like the fucking wind, in and out, leaving nothing but the wreckage behind."

"There's no such thing as a perfect crime," Kerri reminded me, shoving her hands in her pockets to warm them. This place was like a tomb, which was appropriate since so many had died here.

I read once that people who died violently left behind a psychic remnant, or echo of their last moments. I didn't know if it was bullshit but this place vibrated with pain and misery. I didn't know how I missed it the first time around. I'd been too overwhelmed by the grandeur to hear the subtle cries whispering in the darkness of this place.

But I could hear them plain as day now.

"I'm going to wait outside," Dylan announced, spinning on her heel and practically running away. She felt it, too.

Tana had died in this place.

I didn't know how many others drew their last breath between these walls.

One was too many.

Something glinted in the rare shaft of sunlight piercing the ceiling. I moved toward the light, careful where I put my feet, ignoring Kerri's warnings and Hicks' growled protests.

As I moved closer, my heart threatened to stop. I knelt carefully and dug something out of the matted carpet. Something that shouldn't have escaped the eagle eye of Madame Moirai's guards, shouldn't have survived the blaze, and never should've escaped melting in the heat lay in the palm of my hand like a gold-plated beacon of stubborn hope.

The cross Tana had been clutching tightly in her hand, the one piece of personal property Olivia had failed to collect, the one that Tana's grandmother had given her, was somehow in my hand.

Tears sprang to my eyes. How was it possible? The last time I saw it, Tana had hidden it in her palm right as we'd been dragged to the auction. Even drugged, Tana had managed to keep hold of it but somewhere along the way, she'd dropped it and it'd gone unnoticed.

I curled my fingers around the tiny bit of cheap metal and held it to my heart. I wasn't religious or superstitious but I swore I felt Tana's hand on my shoulder as I fought the sob that burned in my chest.

In the craziest way, this necklace represented me.

I would survive against horrific odds, clamp my teeth around Madame Moirai's neck and bring that bitch down — along with every single motherfucker associated with The Avalon.

I'd walked into this place a victim.

I was leaving a predator.

———

EXCITED **for the final book in *The Auction* trilogy? Enjoy an excerpt from THE GIRLS THEY FEAR coming out soon!**

"DON'T GET TANGLED up with Badger, he's bad news," Dylan warned with a dark scowl after I'd clicked off. "Trust me. He's like a cancer. He'll eat you up until there's nothing good left in you."

"I can take care of myself. Besides, we need the money, right?" I asked, slinging my backpack over my shoulder. "I'm supposed to meet him in the back room at the club. Any tips?"

"Yeah, don't fucking go," Dylan answered.

"What the fuck is wrong with you? Ever since we left the auction house you've been different. It's like someone plucked the sense right out of your head. You're the sane one, remember? I'm the irrational fuck-up. Let's keep it that way."

I shrugged, saying, "I call it an improvement," She was right. I did feel different because I was different. Facing the auction house, reveling in its burnt husk, knowing I'd brought it down, poured steel courage down my spine. I wasn't afraid anymore. My fingers found the tiny cross hanging from my neck. "If you want to come along and give me some pointers, that'd be great. Otherwise, cover for me with Hicks."

"That's a turn of events, *me* lying for *you*. I don't like it."

"Life sucks. You coming?"

"You're a dick. Of course, I'm coming. If I don't go, you'll end up getting killed. The streets are rough, especially where Badger runs his business." She slung her backpack over her shoulder, resigned but still pissed. "You owe me."

"You're coming on your own. Don't slow me down." Then, we climbed out the fire escape. Hicks was passed out on the couch from the bottle of Jack he'd started slugging back around three that afternoon. Likely, he was out until tomorrow morning, which worked perfectly.

Badger said the job would only take a few hours. With a little luck, we'd be done and back before Hicks noticed we were gone.

But even if we weren't, Hicks wasn't our dad and he really didn't try to be, *thank god.*

That was the benefit of staying with a disgraced ex-cop turned private detective with demons he couldn't quite slay — he had no room to judge. Kerri was the one who would try to put her foot down but she wasn't here so I didn't have to worry about her.

We stepped into the night, wearing our wigs and hoodies, careful to avoid any CCTV and melting into the shadows. We'd become experts at hiding our faces and avoiding eye contact with anyone.

The thing was, most people didn't want to notice us. We just took advantage of people's discomfort.

We were the throwaway kids, the ones that society had failed, the ones that Madame Moirai had considered easy pickings.

Maybe at one time we had been.

Not anymore.

Kerri was chasing down leads on the mortuary that'd handled Nova's burial and Hicks was researching the title ownership of the auction house in Esterdell, trying to nail down who actually represented Avalon Incorporated so that left me and Dylan pretty much twiddling our thumbs and playing way too much solitaire.

I couldn't handle that much downtime. Not anymore.

Badger was dangerous as fuck and unpredictable but I looked forward to the change of pace. I needed the adrenaline to power my blood to keep me going. At night I dreamed of finding Madame Moirai and stabbing a knife through her black heart but because we didn't know who she was, the person in my dream was like a faceless phantom that kept drifting out of reach.

I always woke angry and frustrated.

That was my current frame of mind — driven and full of rage.

Seemed appropriate given our circumstances.

I turned my grief into something more useful; my fear into fuel.

And Badger, for all his many faults, served a purpose.

If I was running for Badger, I'd have a certain level of protection throughout the city, in the underground, and being a part of the shadows enabled me to listen without being seen.

It didn't matter to me that what I was doing was illegal.

That ship had sailed a long time ago.

All that mattered now? Vengeance.

And nothing would get in my way.

ABOUT THE AUTHOR

J.H. Leigh is a pseudonym of USA TODAY best-selling author Alexx Andria. She enjoys writing about angsty, emotional stories with deep personal impact. You can find her on social media for more information about her books.

"Books are magic."

Manufactured by Amazon.ca
Bolton, ON

DEAD GIRLS DON'T RUN
OR TELL SECRETS

Nicole, Dylan and Jilly may have escaped the horrors of the auction house but they aren't safe.

Madame Moirai has eyes everywhere. There's nowhere the girls can go that can shelter them for long. On the run, with no one to trust, it's just a matter of time before they're found.

Enlisting the help of a disgraced NYPD detective turned private investigator with demons of his own and a sociopathic criminal kingpin, the girls will discover just how far they're willing to go to take down Madame Moirai.

All they have is each other — and a dogged will to survive.

But will it be enough?

ISBN 9798633181302

90000

9 798633 181302